Kyle,
I hope you enjoy
the book.
Tony Haas

SOLOTOYE

Russia

Meadowlark Songs

and Forgotten Wrongs

Solotoye Russia:
Meadowlark Songs and Forgotten Wrongs
Edited by Janet Haas
Cover design by Kate Haas von der Lieth
Cover photo by Kate Haas Photography
Printed in the U.S.A.

Order this title at www.solotoye.com.

Publisher's Cataloging-in-Publication

Haas, Tony, 1946-
  Solotoye Russia : meadowlark songs and forgotten wrongs : a novel / by Tony Haas.
  p. cm.
  LCCN 2007908369
  ISBN-13: 978-0-9801091-0-8
  ISBN-10: 0-9801091-0-8

  1. Women--Russia--Social conditions--Fiction.
2. Immigrants--United States. 3. Russian Germans--United States. 4. Russia--Social conditions--Fiction.
5. Historical fiction.   I. Title.

PS3608.A237S65 2008   813'.6
                QBI07-600300

"… and if not the real story,
then what the story was for me."
from *Ava* by Carole Maso

Acknowledgements

I extend my sincerest thanks to Janet. She encouraged me in every way possible. She understood my itch to write. She provided Virginia Woolf's metaphorical room of one's own. Janet is my wife, friend, and editor. Thanks to my son Isaac for reading the manuscript, for his words of praise and suggestions for improvement. And thanks to my daughter Kate for providing comments, support, and creating the unique cover.

The literary work of Sandra Cisneros, Carole Maso, Jeff Mock, and Virginia Woolf provided notable influence on the structure and writing of this book.

Like magic molecules scattering light waves, Ms. Cisneros' words refract bright and colorful light for new and experienced authors. She projected a scintillating, intelligent beam on my naïve first attempt at writing. Without the model of *The House on Mango Street* and the spare, radiant style of Sandra Cisneros, this book would not have been possible.

Carole Maso is Halloween Night — tricks, layered costume, and treats. Who is she? Knock on her door. Placed carefully, lovingly in extended sack are precious letters of the alphabet, words, lines, music, and imagery — language. She pushes you into a formless, half-moon, eerie night. She tells you to have courage, daring, but off you must go. If you seek answers, try another door. She has questions

— the right questions, tough, and sometimes, scary questions — a treat for every writer. Carole gave me courage to venture into novel's formless night.

You Can Write Poetry says Jeff Mock in his book by the same name. Jeff convinced me. I tried. I practiced within the structure of the novel because Emma was practicing. We tried. Thank you Jeff for showing us how. Thank you for persuading us to try.

Virginia Woolf's counsel, write 'transparent real life' and all that embraces. Go inside, under, and beyond your characters. Let the inner thoughts and emotions of your characters drive the story. Emma's stream of consciousness is as important as her actions in the story.

To paraphrase Virginia, "For 'literary works' are not single and solitary births. They are the outcome of many years of thinking in common, of thinking by the body of the people, so that the experience of the mass is behind the single voice." I extend a symbolic garland to Virginia, and to that 'body of the people,' that 'mass' — recognition, respect ... gratitude.

A special thank you to the American Historical Society of Germans from Russia and Germans from Russia Heritage Society for providing extensive online resources.

Contents

Letter From Russia . Photographs

Dedication

"This Parting Was Well Made"

SOLOTOYE

Russia

Meadowlark Songs

and Forgotten Wrongs

Destiny

Beware! The soviet nurtures colonist vines that seduce, subdue, strangle.

How did a village of four thousand people on the lower Volga River disappear? Did it vanish because the gods predetermined its destiny? If so, how did this calculated course of events affect the people that lived there?

My name is Emma Wasen. I lived in this village for a brief time. I cheat on chores to put thoughts on paper. I glaze my thoughts with color from solar spectrum's palette. I mold them with tone and rhythm as a potter shapes clay. Thoughts — will they help us understand the fate of Solotoye — the village that vanished?

At times, my thoughts wrinkle like last weeks dirty laundry. Occasionally, they soar, teasing my subconscious like string teases a kitten. At the end of the day, I fold all good thoughts carefully and store them neatly in an imaginary trunk. Words, lines, and stories appear. They rise from the churning chest like vapor from river's placid canopy.

In this misty story, metaphorical pieces of language dangle on a somewhat sinuous, temporal line. Random reflections nestle prose and verse. Hang them out to dry. Watch them. Gentle breezes caress them. Wild winds whip them. Make them your own. Stop at words or phrases you like, dislike. Take them off the line. Change them. Live with them. Dream. Discover. Understand.

We gambled unwittingly on the lower Volga River. We sought neither fame nor fortune. Our longing, our reach was pure — dignity, hope, and right. Catherine seduced us. Soviet vines bound and strangled us.

We are gone.

A Little Dignity
Solothurn . Swiss Confederation . 1764

I christened him Alexei Surikov, Russian Agent Surikov. He traveled from his small city apartment in St. Petersburg to the northern cantons of the Swiss Confederation. He dreamed of wealth, position, and power. Some in the cantons anointed him angel. Others cursed him as a Russian devil — buyer of souls. If the needy people gave name and mark, he didn't care. He received payment for each body loaded onto ships bound for Russia. Tsarina Catherine bought human cargo.

Solothurn's government, its nobility, didn't care when citizens emigrated. Commoners in this canton, like those in many of the German states, had little to eat. Many had no homes and only rags to cover their naked bodies. Men unwillingly served in armies and fought in wars they didn't understand. Surikov called Solothurn his little pond of fish. Fish jumped willingly into the Russian's boat. They kissed him for bringing his boat to their shallow and punishing pond.

Surikov radiated youth, energy, and ambition in this dim, exhausted province. Moral poverty dripped from his polished boots. Tsarina Catherine selfishly rewarded those who sent German people to the Russian frontier on the lower Volga River. Agent Surikov dreamed of rubles and a high-paying position in St. Petersburg. If necessary, he would use the influence of his heavy purse to make friends with Russian officials. *Commissar Surikov*, the title sounded good to the young agent.

Solothurn's weak and impressionable souls described Surikov as tall, strong, and handsome, a true Russian, with a dark beard that he groomed continuously. He looked distinguished — like a young commissar.

Surikov ate, slept, and purchased souls at Gelter's Inn and Tavern in the village Solothurn, which lies south of the city of Basel on the Aare River. Surikov, hiding behind worn curtains, scrutinized people in die marktplatz from the open window of his small room. Commoners waved his leaflets in fists that screamed independence, hope, and dignity. Occasionally, secret dreams lightened their worried and burdened faces. Surikov made note of good prospects. Subtle movement of the clock tower caught Surikov's eye as huge black hands sprang to the seventh hour.

"Time to fish," he mumbled. Wound tight like a clock spring, he bounded to the door. Hook was baited. Shallow pond waited.

They stood shoulder to shoulder — scared, desperate, hungry, and ... thirsty. Each night, Surikov bought them ale, which created an unrecognized obligation. Surikov knew well the art of persuasion. Obligation almost always converted the helpless souls.

The tavern was dark. The smoke-filled room smelled of stale beer, cheap tobacco, dirt, and the stink of human flesh. He sat at a small table with his back to the wall. Leaflets, contracts, and ledger lured hungry prospects swimming the shallow, crowded waters. Surikov missed nothing. He made note of everyone who entered while observing those at the bar talking to Herr Gelter. For a few coins each night, Gelter encouraged the men by telling them he too would go to Russia. He lied.

Surikov talked fast, rarely stopping for questions. The hook dangled with tantalizing truths and loathsome lies to catch the hungry fish. He lied to them about where they would live, Russia's beautiful cities like St. Petersburg, or the country where crops grow like wild flowers in a lush meadow. All would inhabit the unsettled, dangerous Russian frontier along the lower Volga River. All would toil endless hours to tame the virgin land. They would till the soil and send food to Russian cities.

He motioned with his hand to the men blocking the door. His hand lashed from side to side as if swatting a fly. He continued lies sprinkled with truth. Pale light from the lantern hanging on the wall behind him struggled to reach the doorway. Smoke and dust wrestled with the yellow stream. Muted, weakened light rested on a hazy figure, a young woman carrying a child. Light settled on them like a warm, soft blanket. The mother and child stood motionless — framed like a photograph in the low, but wide doorway, which was made with round rough-cut trees the size of a small barrel of ale.

As if floating in the dusty, smoky haze, dirty, bare feet ferried the battered woman towards the well-dressed Russian. A ragged cotton-shirt, needing soap and water, coated her upper body. Below her waist, the tattered, soiled material hung lifeless outside her gray skirt. She carried the child on her hip. A tainted fragment of black cloth struggled to hold an abundance of golden, tangled, and matted hair together at the nape of her long neck. Tangled strands reached the small of her back.

Beneath the sweat and dirt, lived a tired, scared, beautiful face, a sad soul, exposed and vulnerable. The child was naked except for a nightshirt too small for the boy. She carried him as if permanently attached to her right hip, leaning to her left.

Surikov stared at her bare feet as she slowly stepped towards him. She pushed her way forcefully through men blocking her way stopping in front of the table. She said nothing. She pretended to read the papers on the table. Agent Surikov tried to introduce himself. He cleared his throat and stumbled through the memorized message — the small part that was true, mostly true.

He finished and breathed deeply. She spoke.

"They said he was killed ... the war ... almost two years now. The baby cries for food and is getting weak. I no longer have milk ... these rags are all we have. Sir, can you take a young woman with child? Can you take us to Rah..." she pointed to the leaflet, "Rusha? I am strong. Will work hard for man. Can birth many more," she glanced at her son. "Take any man — Rusha man, Swiss, old man. Please … Agent … Surikov."

"Yes, I can take … Namen bitte?"

"Langenbach, Anna." He quickly scratched her name in his book not knowing how to spell Langenbach.

"And the boy?"

"Klaus, like his father."

Agent Surikov issued Frau Langenbach instructions mixed with advise — when and where to meet; find a man to travel with, for protection … maybe to marry. He mumbled something about married couples getting more money. She studied the handsome foreigner.

* * * *

"Herr Kleinwald, Friedrich," the large man barked as if giving a command. Agent Surikov scribbled the name as it sounded. Herr Kleinwald grabbed the pen, drew a bold line through Surikov's attempt, and scrolled his name in large, well-rounded letters. The amused agent looked up to see a smug smile on the man's weathered, clean-shaven face. Herr Kleinwald wore a worn military tunic of some kind and black military boots, no longer black except above the ankle. Rough, tan leather on his left boot pulled away from the sole exposing a soiled, thin, gray sock. Thick rope held up soiled pants that were tucked into his boots.

Broad, muscular shoulders strained the seams of his shirt. He carried himself with dignity, the little that remained in this military man — no doubt an officer. A hint of brightness graced his eyes, though his stare was piercing at times. Surikov raised himself in his chair and prepared for battle.

"Sieben kinder," Kleinwald held up both hands with all fingers up on his right hand and two on the left. He pointed to each finger on the right, as if to count, and repeated, "sieben kinder."

"Und Frau?"

Kleinwald nodded, held up one finger, and laughed. Nine bodies. It was worth the battle, the Russian agent said to himself.

"Are you ready to sign?" Surikov asked.

"No, I need information. If we don't like Russia, can we return to Solothurn?"

"Yes. Tsarina will pay your return voyage." An icy stare chilled Surikov. He looked away, but told the large man, "Some have already chosen to return, you know ... homesick."

"We choose where we live?"

"Yes. You choose — city or country. You choose."

"I'm a military officer. I want to join the Russian Army. Is this allowed?"

"Of course, Russia needs intelligent, educated officers. You would have your choice of duty — close to your family."

"You pay travel and food during the voyage?"

"All is paid. Russian government will provide shelter and food until you get settled in your chosen area and work."

"Are we required to pay back this money?"

Surikov emphatically shook his head, "Tsarina Catherine wants good German citizens to populate her country. She has money to pay for ... the right people. You simply list your names and sign. The boat leaves in two weeks from Basel sailing down-river to Bremen. There, you will board a ship that will take you to St. Petersburg. You will be welcomed by the Tsarina," the agent slid the contract towards Kleinwald and held out the pen. Kleinwald surveyed the men standing nearby as if to ask if he should sign. He backed away.

"Major, maybe Colonel, that will be your rank. You learn Russian, Colonel I think," the pen was offered again, but the skeptical man needed to think. This would take several days. The greedy agent was willing to wait for nine bodies.

Kleinwald raised his ale, as if toasting, and mumbled his thanks. He maneuvered through the crowd and camped at the bar with Herr Gelter. Surikov watched Kleinwald for a few seconds. He made eye contact with Gelter and nodded. Kleinwald would get more convincing lies from Gelter.

"Who is ready to give his mark for a new life in Russia?" asked Surikov as he directed his attention to the men surrounding the table. A young man with a rugged, handsome appearance moved to the front surveying the crowded room as if expecting to see someone he knew. A sheathed knife, attached to a thick leather-belt, rested snugly against his left hip. The acrid smell of spent gunpowder oozed from a pistol that was tucked into the man's belt. A large silver buckle adorned the belt. The stranger's eyes shot from side to side. He checked the doorway one more time. He held a quart of ale in his left hand. The right hand rested on the handle of his pistol. Clean clothes and a shaven face marked the man. A full purse tugged at his belt. A thin scar was noticeable on his left cheek.

"I hear papers are not needed. Is this true?"

"Yes. Namen bitte?"

"Herr Zimmer," he checked the doorway again and glanced in the direction of Herr Gelter as if expecting a signal.

"Full name?"

"Luther Zimmer."

"Single?"

"Yes. Single. How soon …" he stole the pen from Surikov ready to sign. "We meet in Basel. Das ist richtig?"

"Yes. That's right."

"When? What date?"

"Two weeks — fourteen, July."

"Did the young woman with child sign? Where is her

husband? She can't make such a long journey alone."

"Her husband died. Yes, she signed. We will take care of her ... unless you ..."

"Agent Surikov, I don't like you. You tell lies for money. This is a dangerous trip for a woman traveling alone. You know it. I will take care of her Surikov." Zimmer signed the paper and slipped through the mass of people ending at the bar. Zimmer handed Herr Gelter a large coin, nodded, and disappeared.

He will never stay, Surikov said to himself. But that was not his concern. Payment was due when he got them on the ship at Bremen. Russian military would guard them during their voyage to the lower Volga.

"It's late gentlemen. Tomorrow, I will be in die marktplatz, then, in the tavern." He gathered his soiled, precious papers and pushed his way through the crowded room.

* * * *

At July's end, Anna and Klaus Langenbach, Luther Zimmer, and the Kleinwald family boarded a ship in Bremen. Agent Surikov weighed his heavy purse as he slithered from the dock. A sneer marked his face as thoughts returned to that little pond in Solothurn.

A year would pass before the Swiss Germans reached their destination on the Volga River, the frontier military post of Saratov. Russian military escorted them across the Volga and ordered them onto wagons. Sixty miles north, the colonists stepped down from the wagons, anxiously scanning their new home, the remnants of a village called Solotoye.

Teased By The Gods
Solotoye Russia . 1900

I remember the sun hanging above the horizon like a celestial pearl veiled by pale-gray morning-mist. Young girls carried water with skirts swaying. Men, women, and children cut and stacked golden shafts of wheat. Mother Nature gently tapped us on our shoulders saying, "Look what I did."

One-by-one, we stopped, hypnotized by nature's simple beauty. We smiled inside and returned to our tasks. A solitary voice in the distance began to sing. Others joined — humming the provincial melody, bursting with song, or simply swaying to the poetic rhythm. Lyrics and music for working and for playing —

My Solotoye, my Solotoye,
Teased by the gods.

Blessed with Matushka Volga and meadowlark song,
They send winters long.
Rich soil on endless grassy plains,
They take away the rains.

My Solotoye, my Solotoye,
Teased by the gods.

Sunrise and sunset beyond compare,
Heat and wind are also there.
Occasional bountiful crops are due.
Untimely locusts eat their way through.

They tell us the tale of Ivan's gold.
The bandit's map they withhold.
A colossal world they provide.
In a box, they make us hide.

My Solotoye, my Solotoye,
Teased by the gods.

Meadowlark song and winters long,
Grassy plain with little rain,
Many things beyond compare,
Heat, wind, cold — ours to bear.

My Solotoye, my Solotoye,
Teased by the gods.

Liquid Grace

I pulled my legs up under my skirt, sat crossed-legged, straightened my spine, and forced my shoulders back. Head rolled in small circles. Arms stretched as if reaching. Toes and fingers wiggled while waiting for the job ahead. My younger brother reproachfully rolled his eyes chiding my antics. I placed my writing board on my lap. Thin, brown string held blank, white paper to the finished board. A small, round bottle sat patiently at my side. Inside clear glass, dense liquid, like thawed coal, welcomed a sharp, absorbing, metal tip. Featherless quill fluttered to my spirited hand wondering where we would … wonder.

Today's exploration was planned days ago. I decided to write about Father, Bernard, and Wolf working. Father told me about their shed-painting project. I thought it a good place to start. I positioned myself afar to thwart any accidental or mischievous splattering of smoky-white paint, yet neighborly to enable painters' mumbling and grumbling to reach attentive, nosy ears. The first messages caught in flared auricles told me that they were not happy painting the shed. They were less happy with me studying them and their work. Wolf expressed his near-anger with my presence in not so subtle ways.

As my father and brothers applied their skills and paint, they transformed an aging shed into a youthful structure, like a building in early bloom. I was amazed at their skills, at how they used their tools — paint, brushes, sharp things used for scraping faded, cracked paint, and other things as well. I studied their tools. I compared them to mine — ink to paint, pen to brush, bottle to pail, paper to shed, well, that's all. Ink is writer's paint, I said to myself. I lingered over the words. I liked them. It pleased my inner ear, so I repeated the novel phrase until it rushed through my veins — until it became a part of me.

I brushed thoughts on used paper as fast as they came to me. I studied my notes and sensed smoothness, form, and suppleness. I create graceful words and lines like my father and brothers create a beautiful new building with their paint. My work is liquid grace. I played with the words. I played with them as a sated feline frolics with its food.

Is it grace as in being graceful, or is it like a prayer — giving thanks at the table, or is it both? Maybe it relates to charm, beauty, love, and charity. I pondered the possibilities and reflected on the relevance. As I meditated, I stared beyond the birch-tinted shed into fruit trees I didn't see. After some time, I decided that liquid grace represents all those things. It depicts ease of movement, rest, and playfulness like a cat. It symbolizes elegance, symmetry, balance, harmony, and rhythm like in a painting or song. It exemplifies refinement, finesse, blessing, forgiveness, mercy, and benediction. My new writing goal emerged. It flowed from my deliberations like … liquid grace. My writing must have grace and all that word expresses or suggests.

Numbness and prickly pain tapped me on my ... Move, get up, do something besides sitting. I pushed myself up, stretched my legs, and massaged my backside to get blood flowing. I brushed dirt from my skirt and waved goodbye to the other workers — painters. In return, I received two almost imperceptible nods and one unforgiving frown.

That night, I dreamed of ravens cawing from birch trees and a strange looking building made of paper covered with black feathers. I stirred. I rubbed my eyes and scratched my head. "Writer's paint ... liquid grace," I mumbled. I smiled and slipped into a restful sleep.

On Sunday afternoon, I gathered my tools and escaped with Peter and Maria to my garden sanctuary behind the church. There, I sat on the ground with my back resting on the west wall of the stone church gazing into Father Thomas' secluded Eden. I stretched my legs in front of me and wiggled my toes. Later, I would hear the men singing from across the road at Wiggens' Place. It's my signal — that it's time to leave. I sensed quiet, lazy, and warmth of a seemingly endless Sunday afternoon. Subconsciously, I monitored the play of my children. Thoughts began to soar on temperate currents teasing the heavens. Father Thomas' prized oleander bushes always inspire and intrigue me. The children know the leaves can hurt them. Interesting that something so lovely can be so dangerous.

Some people are like that. I ponder the notion each time I see them.

I wanted to explore thoughts I had the previous two days — writer's paint and liquid grace. I held the paper containing my notes in front of me as if inspecting it. I ran my fingertips over its surface sensing its smoothness, its character. I brought the paper to my nose and breathed deeply. How do I describe the smell of used paper saturated with fresh ink? I asked myself.

"Whatcha doin' Emma?"

I peaked over the top of the paper and saw Greta's two younger brothers, Heinrich and Jacob, who were peering over the fence looking both puzzled and inquisitive.

"Ah … writing, no … thinking about writing."

"Does your paper smell funny?" asked Heinrich.

"No, not funny, it smells like … I don't know what it smells like," I replied as I motioned with my head for them to join me. "What does it smell like to you?"

They looked at each other, smiled, and made their way around the fence. After each gave the paper a series of serious sniffs, Jacob looked at his brother and then to me. He shook his head and shrugged his shoulders.

"Emma, it smells like paper."

"What kind of paper? It's old paper with ink on it. That has to make it smell different than new paper," I replied.

"Why is it important to know what it smells like

Emma?" asked Heinrich.

"Because these are my ..." I hesitated saying it, "my tools."

"You mean like a shovel, pitchfork, or plow?" asked Jacob, looking puzzled again.

"Yes."

Heinrich sat down and Jacob followed. Maria joined us and made herself comfortable on Jacob's lap. Peter continued digging in the dirt near the fruit trees using hands, heels, and a large stick.

"Writing is my work. Don't you see? You plow, seed, and harvest. I write."

"I'd rather plow than write, and I don't like plowin' much," Heinrich replied. "Writin', well, it's too much like school. Isn't it?"

"And you don't like school?" I asked.

"Hate school. Hate plowin'. Don't like writin'."

"How about you Jacob?" he nodded, agreeing with his older brother.

Two brothers, two years apart in age — they don't look like brothers. Heinrich is tall with a thin face. Jacob is short with a round face like his mother. Both have straight, blackish hair and lots of it. Heinrich's pants are too short ending well above his ankle. Jacob was surely wearing Heinrich's old pants — too long, causing him to roll them several times.

"Emma!" shouted Heinrich bringing me out of my

trance.

"Sorry, I was … thinking."

"About?" Heinrich asked not sure he wanted an answer.

"Oh, I don't know. Last night, I dreamed about a house made of paper. There were ravens and raven feathers on the house. I think it symbolizes my writing. The feathers are black ink, and the house is … I don't know." I stared at Greta's brothers knowing they didn't understand, but they seemed to care, so I continued. "For me, writing is like exploring at the river. You never know what you'll find — maybe a new path, a bird you've never seen before, a snake that frightens you and that is frightened by you, a flower, many things. When I write, I end up on unexpected paths. I discover new ideas and new words. I think critically about different and new things. I learn." Heinrich smiled and nodded.

I continued expressing my wrinkled thoughts. "Anton says I should send my writing to the German paper in Saratov. I think I will … when I get better … when I start to write with grace."

"Grace?" asked Heinrich.

"Yes, liquid grace," I replied as I gazed at pink and white oleander blossoms.

Merry, male voices on River Road severed my silent stupor. They reminded me that the afternoon must come to an averse closing. Peter, hearing the familiar, jovial sounds, anticipated my calling and sauntered towards us reluctantly while retaining his digging tool. His hands, face, and clothes told the tale of his midday toils on this day of rest. Late-afternoon sun cast long shadows on River Road as we headed for our comfortable homes. Heinrich and Jacob nodded as we parted at the southeast corner of the square. Maria and I smiled and waved goodbye. Peter nodded to his male elders — then smiled at his mother. I ruffled his hair and returned his smile.

Bettina . Annette . Anna

My teacher and my friend, Schulemeister Hohgan, said, 'In order to write well, you must read well.' How do I thank Gerhard for finding, buying, and sharing the work of three wonderful women, Annette von Droste-Hulshoff, Bettina Brentano-von Arnim, and Anna Ritter-Knight?

I use their first names because I know them so well. I have read Anna's collection of poems so many times — *Volkslied, Ein Stündchen Lang,* and more. Many lines onto memory etched — Anna's poem about kissing, *Vom Küssen*, *"when I was so young and dumb ..."*

It's a wonder, a miracle, that I can read the words. Their German is so different from our mutated, modified, musty language.

Annette's *Zeitbilder*, vignettes of the times, exposes her struggle for independence and freedom. They show the tension created by her need for tradition, and at the same time, her disdain for it. Freedom lost.

Bettina's *Brief Romane*, letter novels, are poetic feasts. Peck, nibble, or dine. With every bite, the reader tastes a woman that is unsettled and agitated. She is disruptive. Bettina disturbs things. She is troubled and explosive.

We are a society of four — sisters linked not by blood, but allied by kindred personalities, bound by mutual matters, concerns, conditions, and states of being.

Thank you, Gerhard, for expanding my intellectual

world. Thank you Anna, Bettina, and Annette. Your magnetism generates a tenacious tug, a powerful pull. I cling to your courage and to your lyrical language.

Read. Read well.
Write. Write well —
Clear, concise,
Graceful, poetic prose ...
And verse with voice.

Female voices sing, cry, and talk about their times, about seasons of discontent, about concerns, conditions, and states of being. Wunderbar!

Women writing ... writing well.

Old School Papers

I veiled a blushing sixteen-year-old face with shaking hands as familiar words clanged in my ears like a rusty, off-tone, hand-held, school-bell. When I wrote the words, they rang true. They had resonance, meaning, and sweetness. Surely, Schule Meister Hohgan wouldn't read the whole report. I tried to convince myself, but sweetness soured, meaning took flight, and clang, clang, clang.

The schoolhouse was stuffed with parents and students. Naked windows let in a cool breeze and framed fiendish faces of young boys standing outside. Why did I continue to look at them? When not examining and questioning those faces, I surveyed my feet, that I forgot to clean, and hands that refused to stay in my lap. Desperate ideas flooded my consciousness. I tried making myself smaller. I willed myself younger. I attempted a vanishing trick.

I abandoned my futile, childish wishes as thoughts turned to how I got myself into this embarrassing situation. I wanted to get out of doing laundry, other chores, so I convinced Father and Mother that I should stay in school to learn to write ... stories, poems. They reluctantly agreed because I was relentless and persuasive. And, they love me. I had outgrown school as I did many of my clothes. But I continued to wear them because we had little money. I stood head and shoulders above the boys. It never occurred to me to slouch.

'Tell me the story of Solotoye,' Herr Hohgan said. 'Tell me how it smells, tastes, looks, and sounds. Tell me, from your perspective, how it really feels to live day-to-day in Solotoye.' That's what he said. I remember. And so, I filled empty papers with a developing voice.

Now, old and crumpled papers tell the story of my Solotoye. Now, I cover an older blushing face.

Like Solotoye's roads that take us here and there, my school papers are included, here and there, to reveal a Fräulein's perspective of *the village*.

One Village . Many Names

When our ancestors stepped down from their wagons so many years ago, boots and bare feet pressed the soil of a place called *Solotoye*, which was nothing more than scattered remnants of an abandoned village on the road between Saratov and Samara. The emigrants called their new home *Wittmann*, the name of the first elected mayor.

A short time later, the people changed the village name to *Solothurn*, the Swiss Canton where many of the settlers originated. The German-speaking colonists called it *Solothurn*, but the local soviet called it *Solotoye*. And so, we call our village *Solotoye*, sometimes *Solothurn*, sometimes *Wittmann*, but mostly, we simply call it *the village* ... or *home*.

Quiet

The village wears a ragged brown coat the color of dry dusty roads and dirt farmyards — boots like coal — gray pants like an overcast December day — and a faded, white work-shirt.

The sun bakes reds, blues, and greens on shutters and doors until they are pale like the shirt. Yet, these pallid colors, like a cats yellow unblinking eyes staring into lantern's light, shine amongst the dull blacks, browns, and grays.

Solotoye sits quietly, motionless in a rigid wooden rocking chair watching passersby. It shushes those who speak. It scolds the wind when it roars like a lion. It peers relentlessly at roosters crowing, pungently at pigs grunting, and cynically at cows mooing.

I don't like quacking, clucking, baying. Quiet, I like quiet — that's what I'm saying.

Shush.

Quiet please, it would say.

All did obey.

Eerily quiet village,

Like dense forest on a moonless night,

Solotoye lay quiet like hay.

Shush …

Farmyards

The Zimmer farmyard mirrors the Schultz yard — the Schultz yard echoes the Wahl property — and Wahl's bears a likeness to the next. On and on, throughout the village, this one matches that one. Rough fences, thirty paces over and seventy up or down, corral private property and lives. Thankfully, tiny creatures called difference swim in this silly sea of sameness. The lovely and needy people of Solotoye love the sameness. They need the difference.

Double and single houses render the most difference. At least, the outsides do. The big house overshadows the small house. Small house looms over the outhouse. Big and small — one shape fits all. Big measures twenty-five feet wide and fifty feet long. The Zimmer family lives comfortably in the small big-house. Solotoye boasts of its log houses with thatched roofs. Few remain. They are beautiful, but hard to maintain. Most houses wear coats made of wooden planks or clay bricks and hats made of tin. Even with different garments, we take careful account of the yard we're in.

All houses face away from the street. They crouch behind wooden fences and gates with hands over shuttered eyes, like a child playing hide and seek. We separate yards into front and back. The fore is always smaller than the rear. A row of buildings spans the width of the property isolating house area from the great stretch beyond. Sheds with gray weathered-wood, the color of Grandpa's beard, contain wagons and winter's sleds. They anchor the row's left side. Next, we build stalls for horses, cows, and sheep. These well-tended chambers line up straight in a row — not too high — rather low. Close your eyes and smell the familiar fragrance. The noisy chicken coop gets the next spot. It smells of wet feathers and not-so-dry droppings. A granary grabs the next spot in the row. We try to fill it with sacked wheat and rye used for making flour, sacks filled with seed — enough for two seasons, and bundles of grain waiting to be sold at market.

We sprinkle sparingly, like Solotoye showers, about dusty front yards various other creatures. Outhouses demand strategic and social placement. Need I say more? Some prefer to share accommodations with the precious animals. Grandpa says he needs a door. So, we have houses by the score — outhouses and main houses, cookhouses and bathhouses, and still there is more.

Gardens for vegetables, we do keep.
Tomatoes, onions, carrots, peas, are there to reap.
Potatoes, cabbages, blackberries, and more —
Some we eat, the rest we store.

Earthen-domed cellars live in the front yard. Every farmyard has one, sometimes two. They are much more than a simple hole in the ground used to store food. They become little castle-like dungeons — my favorite place to hide — sometimes playing, sometimes not. Double-doors lie on the face of this small mound that looks like the shell of a large, brown turtle. Stone steps take you down to that dark and damp, musty and mysterious, playground. Even with lantern's light, you don't know what's there. If I hold the light in front of me, my backside protests its murky view. I quickly swing the weak beam around. Anything lurking there? It always goes this way — checking corners, straining to see what moved, never still. So why is it my favorite place?

It's a mystery.

It's a thrill.

It's out of bounds,

And summer chill.

A Peak Behind Pallid Blue Shutters

Similarity dwells behind shutters on small big-houses and smaller small-houses. Entries dwarf kitchens where people and things bump into each other. One bedroom indulges the simple needs of the old people. The remaining family sleeps, and everyone eats, in a large room left of the entry. Dining table and benches, sometimes chairs, get tucked into a corner of the large room opposite the kitchen wall.

A wooden ladder inside the vestibule leads to the attic. Dusted and oiled rungs tempt me. Eventually, they transport the curious, sometimes the stupid, higher and higher. Up there, summer's unbearable heat creates a threat of fire. As a small girl, I thought it a good place for hide and seek. I always ventured to the out-of-bounds, but what fun is it if you're never found? With the cry to come in, I finally crawled down that ladder smelling like dust and sweat dripping from my chin. In my hair, an angry spider did crawl. I brought with me its web and all. A fine line, also rarely found, hides between clever and stupid. I still remember laughter, the smell, boredom, and trying to see in the dark like an owl with bad eyes. My head turned looking here and there, but never seeing. Silly things we do.

When Grandma and Grandpa leave us, Mother and Father move into their room. To find it, open the first door to the right after entering the house. Die himmelbett, the heavenly bed, with feather pillows piled high, dominates the simple room. Sometimes, stacked pillows crowd the corner. A curtain hides the feathered and down treasures and protects them from dust. Next to the door, sits a large, reddish-brown, wooden trunk that contains winter and good clothes saved for special occasions. In good times, the family money remains idle and concealed in the recesses of that beautiful piece of furniture.

Sometimes, a couch rests along the wall. There, Grandma and Grandpa take naps, or they sit and stare with hands folded neatly in their laps. There, Grandma and Grandpa pray, or they think of days gone by perhaps.

A painted wooden bench nestles the inside wall of this same room. When not being used, Mother and Father keep their prayer books and rosaries on a simple table next to the bed. Small green plants sit on the windowsills catching the sun's rays when the shutters open. A picture of the Tsar, faded and frayed at the edges, hangs on the wall above die himmelbett. A simple homemade cross rests next to the Tsar's image, inadvertently implying equal importance.

Above the couch on the outside wall, three family photographs cling to rusting nails — Grandma and Grandpa, Mother and Father, and one of Mother, Father and children taken when I was ten. I wore my cousin's dress for the picture because I didn't have anything nice to wear. I looked like a ten-year-old, old lady in the massive maternal frock. It's the only photograph of my brothers and me.

My brothers called me Grandma Ten. That was then.

In a kitchen too small, we have and do many things: large stoves and ovens share heat with each bedroom; a worktable made bigger over the years; unfinished boards on the walls where dishes and foods are kept; spotless pots and pans hang from metal hooks in the ceiling and occasionally lounge on top of the ovens; the cherished samovar used for making licorice tea reigns from a table in the corner looking like a Russian bronze deity.

Shattered Words

Like a hand-me-down winter coat that will always be too big, our new church will never suit Solotoye.

It's big in the shoulders
And wide at the waist.

It has charm. It has grace.
It looks out of place.

It's big. It's pretty.
Ours to wear ... pity.

Father Thomas accepted long ago that he has little connection with his flock. His sermons, though usually well prepared and presented, often rattle around this monstrous building, banging off distant walls and lofty ceiling. When exhausted, they fall to the floor with a whimper. Exiting faithful trample the shattered words. They are swept out on cleaning day.

I kneel on a hard, recently swept, recently oiled, wooden floor.

"These punishing planks are my penance for what?"

Today, Father's raging lecture scorched our ears like blistered prayer.

Checking for spots on my skirt, I ask, "What is his

goal — fear or understanding?"

I encounter no fear. I gain no understanding.

Latin words, I don't understand, float over my head like cotton from trees by the river. I reach for them, to get hold of them. Hopeless.

In Nomine Patris …

His Shirt?

"Psst. Psst. Greta, I have a plan."

I poked her with my elbow, but I received no response. I gave her an exaggerated look of frustration — nothing. I uttered an amplified, "Psssst," trying not to disturb Father Thomas at the altar and the women sitting around us. "I have a plan Greta." She didn't look at me pretending to follow the mass. "Pssst. Greta." I nudged her again. She grudgingly looked at me and shook her head.

"Stop bothering me. I'm praying." She continued staring into her book, but I knew better. Her thoughts lodged permanently, if not devoutly, with my brother.

"Don't you want to hear my plan? It's a good one." Greta shook her head again and turned away from me. She left me no choice. I grabbed the back of her babushka, and I slid it off her head.

"Stop it," she whispered, giving me a disgusted look — but with a half-smile. "Tell me after mass." She replaced her head covering while holding onto the knot below her chin.

Everyone around us stood. Greta and I did the same without thinking. Father Thomas and two altar boys were busy doing … saying … something. I returned my attention to Greta.

"No. I might forget," I said too loudly.

"Shsshh!" Frau Wittmann poked me in the back with

her bony finger. I furled my eyebrows at her. I could do nothing more ... at least without being disrespectful.

My Sunday morning mood controlled me. I don't understand why this happens, but I secretly enjoy it. I pinched Greta's nose with my thumb and forefinger, and I pulled her head towards me. I held her nose shut until she had to open her mouth to breathe. I got her to smile. Sometimes, I like being silly — even at age twenty-two. A wife and mother can be silly. Maybe, they should be silly on Sunday?

"This is what we're going to do. I say we go to the tavern this afternoon, and we drink with the men." I felt bony fingers again, but I ignored them. Greta stared at me with a bewildered look. She shook her head. I nodded emphatically.

"No," she whispered.

"Yes, we are." Again, I spoke too loudly because Father Thomas turned and looked in our direction. I quickly held up my rosary, so he could see it. I crossed myself pretending to finish the last decade. He knows me too well. I saw him shake his head as he followed the altar boys out of the sacristy. "Now, we can talk Greta."

"Outside," she whispered as she moved from the bench, genuflected, and hurried to the back of the church without me. I watched her take holy water. She anointed her forehead, chest, left and right shoulder. Greta always does this slowly, devoutly. I don't know why this is important to her. I don't think I ever asked her.

I followed Frau Wittmann towards the welcomed golden light coming from the opened doors. She stopped and dipped her fingers into the water. I half-heartedly reached for the fountain, but I missed. "Oh well," I said smiling at my obviously disgusted and uncompromising elder. Greta waited for me on the steps. She looked disturbed. She looked angry. She looked a little like Frau Wittmann. I smiled inside.

"What were you doing in there?" she asked.

"This is my best plan ever Greta."

"I'm not going to the tavern Emma. Don't ask."

"Of course, you're going."

"No. I'm not! I'm not doing it Emma. Our fathers will be there, and ..."

"I know. Anton will be there too. That's what makes it fun. All the men will be there. Wolf will be there."

"No, that doesn't make it fun. It makes it foolish, childish. Do you really think the men will let us stay and drink with them?"

"Of course, they won't let us stay. We want to let them know the women of Solotoye deserve to have some fun too. A few hours on Sunday to drink with the men — is that too much to ask Greta?"

"It's not too much to ask Emma. It's too much to expect."

I studied my best friend, and I knew she was right.

"You're right. It is too much to expect, but we still have to do it. I don't have any money to buy a drink. Do you?"

"Emma, it doesn't matter if I have money. I'm not going."

"If you go with me, I'll talk to Wolf again." I smiled and raised my eyebrows.

"Emma, you know that I would do anything … almost anything, to get your brother to marry me, but your talks don't seem to do any good. Do they?" I stared at Greta thinking of what I could say. My silence was too long. It scared her. "See. I'm right. My God, I'm right. There's nothing I can do. He will never ask me to marry him. Tell me I'm wrong Emma."

"You are wrong Greta. Wolf is twenty now. He's getting older. Well, not mature yet, but … We just need a new plan." I pulled Greta down with me as I sat on the top church step. "We need help."

"What do you mean? Who?"

"Maybe, Wolf will listen to Bernard."

"Why Bernard?"

"Older brother — he respects Bernard. He knows Zees and Bernard are happy. Bernard is always happy, but Wolf sees them as a happy married couple." Greta didn't respond. I put my arm around her shoulders. "You need to give it time Greta. It will be fine."

Greta pulled away from me looking into my eyes. "So, the tavern, huh? I love your crazy ideas Emma Wasen."

"Greta, I have another idea." Greta's head dropped. She stared at her shoes waiting for the worst. "I think we should go to the tavern, AND we should wear our hair down. I'm tired of wearing my hair in a bun. Why do we have to wear our hair like our mothers? It's time for change. The men like our hair down in the bedroom. I feel sexy with it down. Don't you? That's not a sin. Is it? Oh, who cares? I don't think it is, and that's good enough."

Greta smiled. "It's like wanting to wear Wolf's shirt," she said softly while looking around to make sure we were alone.

"What?"

"Emma, I lie in bed at night, and I think of him. I picture his blue eyes, funny half-smile, and broad shoulders." My best friend was confiding in me, but she was talking about my younger brother. I tried to hold back the laughter. I turned away pretending to watch jays in a nearby apple tree. I wiped away a tear.

"I feel his rough, strong hands. I recall his scent. Emma, I think about wearing his shirt in bed — just his shirt — nothing else. I feel sexy, like you wearing your hair down. You know, for Anton when ..."

I couldn't hold in the laughter. It rushed out, reckless and loud, like boys from the schoolhouse. Greta looked at me, horrified. "I'm sorry Greta."

"I thought we were sharing. I hate you Emma Wasen."

"Greta, you're two whiskers away from … from wobbly."

"What? Two what … ?"

"You know. You're unstable like a cat without whiskers … crazy … I don't know. It just came out. Greta, I'm sorry, but he is my brother. It sounds funny when it's your younger brother."

"So, you think I'm crazy — two whiskers away?"

"Yes … I mean no. You're in love. I understand. I do!" I hugged her. "I love you Greta Buchs, soon to be Greta Buchs Zimmer." She smiled. "It's settled then. We go to the tavern this afternoon, and we wear our hair down. I'll come by after chores."

When Greta was far enough away that she couldn't hit me, I yelled to her, "HIS SHIRT?"

I yanked up my skirt, and I started running.

Tavern's Gate

The sign simply reads Wiggens' Place,
But it says so much more.

It says welcome
To the tired men of Solotoye.
It says hello.
You have a friend here.

It says relax,
Enjoy warm Zhiguli beer from the barrel,
Rodnik vodka by the glass
While you sit on benches made of wood
Under a roof made of grass.

Touch the sign when you enter
For good luck.
Touch the sign when leaving.
Good luck.

Hair Down Bottoms Up

I stopped running a short distance from my house — the Wasen house. I can't be six there. I don't want to, but I can't. I left a home where I could be six if I wanted to be six. Friends call us *the poor but happy Zimmers*. My father drinks too much and Mother can't change that. Maybe she doesn't want to change him. Father doesn't like farming. Artistic creative endeavors inspire him. Maybe that's why he allows me, encourages me, to write. I love him dearly.

My wonderful husband, Anton, our two children, Peter and Maria, my caring and special father-in-law, Konrad, and a mean mother-in-law, Mother Wasen, wait for me at the Wasen house.

Friends and some family call Anton and me *the beautiful family*. Our children are cute, but most children that age are. I describe Anton as the most handsome man in Solotoye. In a teasing way, Anton describes me as not unattractive. That's good, because I feel uncomfortable when people call me beautiful. Call us the happy family, *the happy Wasen family*.

As I helped Mother Wasen with our usual Sunday noon meal of pork, brei, and mashed potatoes, I thought about Greta and me at the tavern. I needed an excuse to leave the house. Mother Wasen will watch the children. Surely she will agree to such a small request. I tried to convince myself. I'll take one or two coins from the jar hidden under quilts and bedding in the big trunk at the foot of the bed. Anton knows exactly how much is there. He will miss whatever I take. I pictured him carefully counting and recounting. I scratched my head and smiled.

Anton gave me a loving pat as he left for the tavern. He noticed the smile. Glancing over his shoulder, looking puzzled, he ran into the door. A playful, loving smile still lightened my face. I felt roguish. I watched him close the door as he rubbed his nose.

I tossed a wet dishcloth in the direction of its hook — missing badly. I bounded to the bedroom like a cat playfully jumping plants in the garden. I released my hair from its monotonous knot and tried combing out the tangled mess.

"Peter, Maria, be good for Grandma Wasen."

Peter asked, "Mother, why are you smiling? Did you think of a joke?"

I nodded. "Your father makes me laugh." Peter and Maria smiled and waved goodbye. *The happy Wasen family*, I thought.

I felt good about how I looked. I felt free ... relaxed. Thoughts of bathing at the river and preparing for bed entered my mind ... hair down.

I left our yard ambling through dusty, empty streets. With each airy step, swaying strands of hair brushed my thin cotton-shirt. Small coins jingled in the pocket of my skirt. Light and carefree suddenly changed to weighted worries. I breathed deeply, and I forced a smile. I concentrated on bouncing like a cat. I chose not to skip because … well, cats don't skip.

My pace slowed and my smile faded as I approached Greta's stone house. I swung my head slightly as I knocked. My hair moved gracefully ... childlike.

Closed shutters and closed door did not bid welcome. I knocked again. I heard footsteps and Greta telling her mother she would answer the door. The door jerked open.

"Greta, your hair … it's suppose to …" I pulled a few, still tangled, tresses to the side — reminding her. "Hair down, remember?"

"Not here." She pushed me off the stairs. The door slammed shut behind her. "I'll do it when we get to the tavern. Let's go." We rushed through the gate and onto the road.

"This is going to be fun Greta. We are probably the first women to do this."

"I'm quite sure that we will also be the last," replied Greta with an anxious tone.

"I only have a few kopeks. How much do you think a glass of vodka costs? We can order a Zig from Zees like the men. She's going to die when she sees us stride into the tavern with hair swaying."

"I don't know Emma. I don't think money is our real concern."

I looked at Greta, and I shrugged. "We must do this."

"What if Wolf gets mad, and he never speaks to me again?"

"Oh Greta, Wolf never says much anyway. Who would notice?"

"That isn't funny." Greta walked slower and slower as we approached Wiggens' Place. I took her by the arm pulling her forward. We stopped at tavern's gate. I checked my skirt and blouse as fingers tussled with tassel-like hair.

"Greta, your hair, you promised to ..."

"No. I didn't promise."

"Let me help you." I knew Greta wasn't ready for this, so I loosened her hair. She reached in her pocket and pulled out a comb. We giggled quietly like two schoolgirls misbehaving in the back of the schoolroom. I reached for the gate and pulled it open — slowly. I shoved Greta in and closed the gate … without making a sound. I tiptoed along the narrow boardwalk with Greta in front. I nudged her forward. I whispered in her ear, "Smile and act like we belong here. Watch the nails. You don't want to …"

She responded in a flash, "We don't belong here, and I can feel your sweaty palm on my back."

"Why doesn't Push fix this crazy boardwalk?" I asked.

We saw them before they noticed us. The male-populated background blurred. I couldn't see anyone or anything clearly. A fuzzy, pillar-like image of Zees stood erect, but motionless, amongst tables and men. I blinked hard trying to clear my eyes. Somehow, I managed to spot an empty table. I grabbed Greta's hand, and we moved slowly, cautiously in that direction. My heart pounded uncontrollably. I must say something. I must tell them why we invaded their tavern, but I could barely swallow. How could I speak? Talking and laughing stopped abruptly. Rough, hairy hands held drinks frozen in odd, frightful contortions. Zees dropped a tray of empty glasses causing Stay to hiss. He darted from under the table. In a blink of my blurry eyes, he disappeared around the corner of the distant shed.

I don't remember getting to the table. We sat facing puzzled and angry faces. I saw unfriendly features and glaring white eyes. The silence was terrifying. Zees picked up tray and glasses, and she sat them on the table. She moved towards us. Her movements appeared slow, fuzzy. I heard her footsteps. I felt pounding in my chest. Out of the corner of my eye, I saw Greta staring at me. Her eyes screamed anger and fear. She, no doubt, contemplated a quick exit.

"What are you doing here? Your hair! Emma! Emma, look at me." I forcefully pulled my eyes from those angry faces. "You are one crazy woman Emma Wasen, and I love you for doing this," said Zees quietly as she flashed a big smile. "What can I get you to drink?" she asked.

"NO! No women, men only," yelled Herr Mueller from the table next to us. "The tavern serves men. You see, MEN." He motioned emphatically with both hands. "Wasen, your wife belongs at home." I started to get up to tell old man Mueller what I thought of his opinion, but Zees and Greta pulled me down signaling me to stay quiet. "Zimmer, you spared the rod on this one. See what happens when you spare the ..." My father and husband jolted from their seats in unison ready to defend themselves against Mueller's attacks.

"STOP," yelled Push. He motioned for Anton and Father to sit. "It's my tavern Mueller, and I welcome the women. Zees, get the ladies what they want."

Mueller retorted with anger. Spit flew from his mouth. "If they stay, I leave." He pushed himself away from the table finishing his vodka. He faced us shaking his finger as if reprimanding a child. He backed into Father's table, caught his balance, if not his composure. I heard the gate slam shut. I took a deep breath. After an uneasy silence, Zees asked again what we wanted to drink.

"Zees, we don't have much money. Bring what's cheapest," I whispered. Feeling self-conscious and less than confident about my hair, I pulled it off my shoulders leaving long strands resting on my back.

"Two vodkas for my friends," said Zees loudly so the men could hear. I smiled at Zees, but I noticed Greta had not moved. She was locked in eye contact with Wolf. She wasn't blinking. I wasn't sure she was breathing.

"Greta!"

"What?" Greta turned her head towards me, but her eyes were still on Wolf. "Oh, yes. I'll have vodka Emma." Zees and I laughed — quietly.

It seemed like forever before Zees returned with the vodka. I pulled the small coins from my pocket, and I handed them sheepishly to Zees while watching for my husband's reaction. His eyes spoke to me — pride, surprise, and a few things I couldn't identify. Zees raised her glass. I lifted my glass trying to steady shaking hands. I nudged Greta. She copied us.

"To the women of Solotoye," Zees blurted then downed her drink.

"To the women of Solotoye," Greta and I repeated with little strength in our voices, but with much conviction. Push picked up the toast. A few men followed. We raised our glasses to the men. I smiled at Anton, and I wiped my moist eyes and cheeks with my sleeve. Wolf didn't join the toast. He stared blindly at the table as he moved his glass in small circles. Greta studied his behavior. Her face flushed with disappointment. I instinctively held her hand.

Father motioned for us to join them. Anton and Bernard smiled. Anton's eyes rested pleasantly on my hair. I let it swing over my shoulder, and I watched hopefully until his eyes met mine.

"Come. Come join us," they said together. Wolf continued to sulk.

I sat next to my husband. Greta defiantly moved to the

other side of the table next to Father — across from Wolf and Bernard. Anton spoke first.

"Greta, I expect this kind of behavior from my wife, but you … you're a respectable young lady. What are your parents going to say?"

Her reply, the strength of her voice, surprised me. She stared at Wolf as she spoke.

"I don't care what they say." We all knew it was a lie, but it didn't seem to matter. "A twenty-one year old woman in this new century does as she pleases. If the elders, and some young men, don't like it, they will have to get used to it." Wolf looked up with penetrating eyes, but he didn't speak. Greta returned a piercing stare, and she ran a hand slowly down her hair. She dared Wolf to respond.

My father noticed the tension, so he put his arm around Greta's shoulder. "You're right Greta. Do as you please. Zees, more vodka, please." Father laughed, saying, "That's a good rhyme — almost as good as, Zees! Got Zig? Das ist gut. Ya?" I watched Father as he protected Greta. I admire his respect for women. He treats me the same as Bernard and Wolf. He considers Mother his equal. We need more men like Father, I told myself.

We drank much. That afternoon we talked about ancestors, about crazy rules of the Kontor, about too little land and not enough rain. We talked about going to that country across the ocean — America. We talked about needing hope. We talked about freedom.

Bernard repeated my final toast, "To hair down," as he put his arm around Zees.

Father smiled, pointed his glass to the three women, and shouted, "Bottoms up!"

It Feels Like Spring
But That's Not The Whole Thing

Solotoye feels like spring,
But that's not the whole thing.

It's comfortable. It's boring.
It's sweet. It's sour.
A challenge, a curse,
Weather changes by the hour.

A wedding, a christening,
Children at play,
Summer's solstice,
A long and sweet day

Harvest, a picnic
And caught in the rain
Swinging, holding hands
A chorus or refrain

Feels like spring
Not the whole thing

Squeezed into a box
Not free
Glass walls tempt us
We see

Turn and go the other way.
Confused, belittled,
Not knowing what to say

Are we Russian,
Or are we not?
Inside the glass box,
Happy and not.

Like spring
Not the whole thing

Larks In The Meadow
Plows In The Field

People of the land
Muscle and calloused hand
Guide the plow
Horse, ox, and camel
At their command

Ribbons of turned earth
Moisture and heat
Mother Nature
Grains given birth

A dog's playful bark
Harvest
Rejoice with song
Like the meadowlark

Larks in the meadow
And plows in the field
Men, women, and children relax
In the granary, bountiful yield

Little Things That Cost So Much

The soviet provides a general store
A scary man guards the door
Things we cannot make
Things we cannot take

Little things that cost so much
Little things of such and such

Many rubles for the pretty dish
Purse is empty, so I make a wish
Always check the pretty dress
How to get Father to say yes

Little things that cost so much
Little things of such and such

Twine and rope on the wall
White string in a ball
Clay marbles from the bin
Beyond the door, a grin

Little things that cost so much
Little things of such and such

Tawny Tabby

Over time, I began to notice, and others would point out similar physical and personality characteristics I share with Stay, Push Wiggens' cat. Push calls Stay a favorite of nature — blessed with good looks, a handsome feline, smart, strong, a fast and fearless hunter ... yet playful. He warms quickly with friends. Strangers scare him. He senses danger in people and situations. I continue to sharpen this skill with Stay's help.

Like a fighter, Stay shows signs of battle. He lost one of his upper fangs in a late-night fight. Because of the missing tooth, his upper lip sometimes gets stuck, and he gets this silly looking curl to his lip. I haven't lost any teeth yet, but friends do say I have a tendency to fight. When I lose, I stick out my lower lip ... pouting.

Short, white hair tips each big paw. I have large feet for a woman. He has tufts of white hair sticking out between the pads on each paw. I don't have anything like that.

Like me, Stay doesn't like it when people laugh at him. He finds a place to hide, to be alone, to sulk when that happens. I usually go to the cove. Stay bounds here and there, chases, plays, hunts, and jumps to catch a butterfly. He also needs his rest. So do I.

He is self-reliant, a thinker, individualistic, aloof. Claws come out when cornered. In these situations, friends respectfully call me callously cruel. I never hiss.

Stay likes to stare at people and into the distance. Who knows where? He loves to have a good time, curl up for a nap with paws and nose tucked under chest — bushy tail wrapped for warmth. Anton thought it funny those first nights together.

They say I'm meddlesome and interfering.
Unfortunately, it's true.
I have company.
Stay does it too.

There's lying around time.
I'm jealous in this regard.
He gets ample lazy time.
I try, but it's hard.

As a gangly kitten,
Farmyards he did roam.
With little encouragement,
He would follow me home.

Many nights he would stay.
Living with an animal still wild,
It's exciting, dangerous.
Does Anton think of me this way?

Dress Like Them Feel Like Us

A colonist, a foreigner
An enemy of the state
A German, a Russian
People they choose to hate

Pants tucked into tall black-boots
Belted white-cotton tunic-shirts
Babushkas
Difference that hurts

Dress like them
Feel like us

Long, flared sheepskin-coats
Short-billed caps or hats
Cloches, Galoshes

A farmer, a miller
A producer of food
A German, a Russian
Why so rude

Dress like them
Feel like us

Sticker Patch

They, the Russians,
Call local government a soviet.

It's a pretty word.
It's an ugly thing.

Like the insufferable sticker patch,
It seems to spread with ease.

We thought their Instruktions were silly,
Only meant to tease.

Now we know better.
They expect us to follow them —
To the letter.

Bow . Obey . Surrender

"Of course, I don't agree with the soviet's rules Emma. They make my job impossible. I shouldn't say this, but I don't like my job. I like being a priest, but I don't like receiving constant instructions."

Father Thomas turned to me. His eyes begged for understanding. "They don't want us to think. We must simply obey, bow down, genuflect, … surrender to their demands. They pay. I dutifully obey." He dropped his head, as if ashamed, and moved freshly turned soil around with dusty shoes — first the right, then the left.

While studying the marks he was making in the soil, he changed the subject and continued. "Emma, did you know we still use farming methods they taught the original colonists? One hundred thirty years without change — we need better farming methods."

"I think the men do a good job raising crops. It's not their fault that we get little rain, that the sun is unbearably hot in summer, that the wind …"

"Yes, they do, but they could do more. I read in the paper some time ago about a man in England who developed a new way of farming. We should use his method. He found ways to retain moisture in the soil, better ways of plowing, and … there were other things as well."

"Have you talked to the men about this?"

"I've tried, but …"

"But what?"

"They don't listen. They don't trust me because I work for the soviet. I'm sure they ask themselves how a priest could know anything about farming."

"You should try again. Talk to Push. He can persuade the men to change. They listen to him. Do you still have that paper?"

"Yes, but ..."

"Ask Push to read it to the men."

"He won't. Push doesn't like me."

"I think you're wrong Father. Push does like you. He teases you because ... I think he is a little jealous of your education. This is important Father. Ask him."

Father Thomas slipped his hands in his pockets and scanned the heavens as if looking for a sign.

I sensed that it was time to move on with the conversation. "Rules — I dislike them all." Father let out a muffled snort. "You're right. Everybody knows that I don't like rules. And that I don't obey many. One rule that really bothers me is no music in the village. The soviet says that music leads to immorality in young people. Of course, we don't follow that rule."

"We don't follow many of the rules, but they still exist. Remember how boys and girls were not allowed to stay out after nine o'clock? If caught, the elders were forced to arrest them and put them in the Budki. At daybreak, innocent boys suffered embarrassing and painful public lashes. We managed to eliminate that rule. I guess things improve with time."

"Father, eliminating idiotic rules is not improvement. We forced them to admit to a mistake."

"They still enforce travel restrictions. I must get approval, in writing, from Shishkin when I need to go to Saratov. I would love to go across Matushka to explore and hunt the Volga Hills, but we can't go there. Ridiculous."

"I don't like talking about this — rules for travel, rules for farming, music, punishment of crimes ... what they think are crimes, how we elect our village leaders, how and when we go to church, duties of our priests ... and as my father likes to say, when we shit and how much. Ooops! Sorry Father."

"Like father ... like daughter. That really wasn't an ooops. Was it?"

"No. Must I confess that one?"

Father Thomas managed a weak smile, but he didn't answer.

"Talk to Push Father. I know he likes you. I think he respects you. He can be a little insecure at times. The men need to know."

Father gave me a fatherly pat on the head and shuffled away — staring at the ground — hands in his pockets.

"They need to know," I mumbled.

Imitation Rain

In Solotoye, we tolerate playful imitation rain. Our showers are tardy, tired, light as goose down, half-wet. A lonely and timid drop plops a weak warning. I carefully feel the top of my head. A solitary, make-believe, funny-looking cloud wandered aimlessly into our village. I watch it with amusement. I try not to laugh. It's like a child trying hard to cry, but the tears don't come — nothing. I watch. I wait.

I look closely and curiously. I observe drops being pushed out against their will. I follow them down one at a time. I hear silly screams until they explode on dry land sending round puffs of dust magically into the air. I glance here ... there ... everywhere around, and I tally dark spots on the ground — one ... two ... wait ... wait ... three ... over there ... four. No need to run for cover. It's only a half bother, like fake rain. It's fake stuff, I say. It's mostly fluff — fake stuff.

I smell dust and listen to plops on the slanted roof of our shed. It's a much different sound than on my head. I watch dainty drops dripping from the roof. Down they go. Together, they etch a line in the ground. Rivulets start to form between patches of dusty earth. They seek low places as if they know what they are doing. I know they pretend.

I follow to make sure they don't get lost. The muddy

stream eventually slips and slides unknowingly into the street. It joins friends in a rut that appears headed in the right direction.

I see drops looking at each other with wide eyes. "Where are we going?" they question anxiously.

A tiny leaf and twig join them in a race downstream — bumping into banks and each other.

Plop, plop, plop. It sounds like fingers tapping a ripe watermelon. Plop, plop, plop.

Little, funny, pretend cloud gives up. He throws up his hands in disgust, and he opens wide to abandon his wanting weight. In one blink, it's over — a sigh from above.

Raging rivulets expand into muddy, stormy streams. They rinse the roads and head for Matushka. Wanting to see them off, I continue my westward trek.

Particles of sand become disagreeable passengers. Gritty silt deposits form at sharp turns.

Matushka's sandy cove tickles droplets as they run to the shore. I hear giggles.

Leaf and twig stop to rest.

I didn't see who was best.

Silly shower slips into Matushka with glee.

Mother Volga asks, "Is this all you have for me?"

Plop.

Wiggens' Wayward Walk

Open tavern's gate
Behold what lies before you
Take caution and be late
As wise men do

Wood permanently borrowed or stolen
Boards sort of lined up
Sort of nailed down

Rusty nails sticking up
Trying to bring you down
Curves right
Juts left

Bent and broken when new
Subject of jokes
More than a few

Too narrow to run
Too wide to miss
So weak — so unsound
So smart to stay on safe ground

Wiggens' Wayward Walk
Too wrong to be right
Too right to be wrong

Guarded Conversation

Commissar Shishkin peers over his shoulder. The short bill of his tilted Russian-Army hat masks one dark gaping eye. Long and stringy hair, the color of pitch, crawls from the hat resting on a soiled collar. Olive-colored skin, oily and wrinkled, compliments his ill-pressed and shiny uniform. He moves closer to Buchs as he checks his back again. Their shadows drop off the weathered table, slither across straw-covered ground, resting on Wiggens' wooden shed. Lantern-light projects black images on gray wood. They huddle over half-empty vodka glasses guarding their conversation.

Shishkin jabs Buchs in the arm repeatedly whispering, "You must convince them to stay. We can't have another mass emigration to America. You know what that will mean. Right? You know. Right?"

Buchs nods and stares at their shadows while thinking how much he detests that military hat and the small, greasy man wearing it. He empties his glass.

"Convince them to stay," Shishkin whispers.

Buchs leaves without answering.

Shadows On Weathered Wood

A solitary, low-pitched, somber tone rolls off the belfry's bronze bell, slow like sap oozing from a pine, sticking on the moist evening air. Another follows. Long pauses irritate. Bong ... bong ... We wait for the next toll ... the next rain ... for crops to grow. We wait. The evening bell tolls six times. At noon, the bell peals punishing penance ... enough for a lifetime of sins.

As the final punishing note wafts over the village and vanishes, three simple souls slip from their farmyard below whirling windmills and amble to the tavern. It's a penitent's pilgrimage. Their pace is set by the bell's resonating cadence. Patrons confess trespasses to the tavern keeper who dispenses endless understanding and forgiveness. When this public admission of sin is not enough to purge their souls, they drink until drunk ... drink to forget. Father Thomas blesses this secular cleansing ritual not with prayer, but with vodka.

"What tales will Wiggens tell tonight?" asks my father, Jacob, of his two sons. He doesn't expect an answer. He doesn't get one. The two young men simply shrug their shoulders in unison and continue on — step by slow sticky step. Like caring guards protecting their charge, Bernard and Wolf frame their father.

Bernard, his wife, Zees, and their children, four-year old Walter and two-year old Helga, live in Father's house.

Our mother, Anna, cares for the children when Zees toils outside the house. Bernard's big muscular frame and un-shaven face disguise his sweet and peaceful nature. Zees labors at home, in the fields, and at the tavern. She is the daughter of Push Wiggens. Zelma Wiggens Zimmer liked it when I started calling her Zees. Everybody uses her nickname. Zees does most of the work at the tavern because Push passes the time telling stories, parting with village gossip, or reading the German paper to the men while they enjoy smoking their long pipes and drinking.

It doesn't bother Bernard that Zees works while he sits night after night socializing. It annoys Zees, but she says nothing. All women in Solotoye do more work than the men, but they say ... nothing. Few men recognize the situation. Why would they? Zees earns a few kopeks that help Father and Mother buy food items they cannot produce. After Bernard has a few glasses of vodka, he enjoys gazing at Zees as she moves from table to table with ankle-length skirt swaying. Bernard accepts other men looking at his wife. Little bothers Bernard. He trusts Zees, and she handles the men well. Her intelligent eyes, attractive face, and demeanor speak to the men. Her size and brassiness intimidate the less confident men.

My younger brother, Wolf, short for Wolfgang, turned twenty a few weeks ago. He works in the village tobacco plant when not needed in the fields or for chores at home. I describe Wolf as boyishly handsome with thick dark hair and with the mature build of a much older man. Wolf mimics his brother in size, but he is more slender and his shoulders are more square than rounded. His natural presence quietly and confidently tells other men — don't mess with me. Bernard and Father ignore Wolf's bearing. Young girls yearn for his attention. They consider him adorable. Unfortunately, Wolf's self-image, occasionally, rivals the girls' yearnings.

Normally, September quietly fans our dry dusty streets. This early-fall day, a rare shower dampened the dust. In places, small puddles formed. Sparrows quickly used the low spots for bathing. The three men shuffle along their usual route. They sidestep the shallow pools trying not to disturb the small birds as they splash intently. Father carries his prayer book and rosary as usual while Bernard and Wolf pretend they don't care. It's one of Father's peculiarities. Tonsured hair, book, and rosary give Father a monkish appearance, which he likes. He totes book and beads in his left hand keeping the right free for vodka. Father thinks nothing of it. The family considers his singularity amusing, silly, and sometimes depraved — depending on our moods.

The men step out in silence towards the village square taking a subconscious and gratuitous bearing on the church steeple. The dominant church and belfry sit majestically on the square's southeast corner. The sanctuary's open doors welcome all travelers at the meeting of Little Karman and

River Road. Around fall equinox, when the sun slides past twelve bells, the steeple's undressed wooden cross accepts the sun's golden gift, sending a ghost-like Calvary image onto warped crossing roads. West of our rural cathedral, rectory and schoolhouse sit in divergent triviality competing for morning sun. The unnamed street on the west of the square boards the general store and the soviet's office — both are meager in appearance but busy. Nestled in the northwest corner of the square is the favored Wittmann farmyard. The remainder of the square consists of well-attended grounds, including Father Thomas' garden located behind the church.

From the back of the church, while hiding in the garden, one can throw small rocks across River Road, and occasionally, hit the swinging sign at Wiggens' Place. On Sunday, the village monitors its pulse by the constant flow of thirsty patrons in and not-so-thirsty patrons out of the secluded tavern, which opens every day except when Push goes to market to buy vodka and beer. Tables and benches fill quickly on Sundays and holy days. Many sit comfortably on the ground. The shed and trunks of the fruit trees provide support for weary backs.

As Father, Bernard, and Wolf turn the corner onto River Road, they notice Father Thomas leaving his garden — apparently talking to himself. The four men acknowledge each other. The Zimmers doff caps in respect for their parish priest. Father Thomas nods his recognition, and he playfully salutes them with a folded-paper in hand.

"Tonight," Jacob mumbles, "I will talk to our young priest about America."

The unlikely location of the tavern, across from the church and rectory, defies its popularity. At first, the meeting place accommodated only a few of Push's close friends. They came to share a drink and to listen to Push's stories. Some of the men boast to neighboring villages that Push is the best storyteller in all colonies. Push never corrects them.

Not many men in Solotoye read German as well as Push. He loves to share his paper with anyone interested. He struggles with many words, but he feels no shame in skipping over or pronouncing words in any way he sees fit.

Father Thomas unlatches tavern's gate. He reaches up, nudging the sign over the entryway, making it swing slightly on its rusty and creaky chain. The flat birch board reads *Wiggens' Place*. Blacksmith Miller burned the lettering into the rustic wood. The men consider it bad luck not to touch the sign while entering and leaving the tavern. Some nudge it. Some push to make it swing. Herr Braun, who is short, fat, and mean hits it briskly with his cane. Most miss it when they leave.

As Father Thomas saunters the short distance from the gate towards the back of the farmyard, he marvels at the double line of fruit trees that curtains the rest of the property. A crooked boardwalk lumbers towards the tavern stopping abruptly at the edge of the thatched awning that protects the men from sun and occasional rain. A new lantern hangs on a leaning makeshift lamppost, which is centered amongst the four long tables that sit beyond the grass awning. A mixture of sand and straw covers the damp ground.

Push opens the sheepskin purse hanging from his wide, thick, tattered cowhide-belt. An added hole lengthens the already-generous leather sash. He drops a few silver kopeks inside his purse. The clinking sound pleases him when the count is small. It delights him when full. He watches Commissar Shishkin and village supervisor Buchs sitting at the far table next to the shed. They drink heavily, but they manage to keep their conversation guarded from the other patrons, and to Push's dismay, from him.

Zees moves gracefully among the tables picking up empty bottles, shot glasses, and any remnants of rye bread or other food. She subconsciously checks her pathway. Stay expects her to go around him when he blocks her way. She turns up the lantern's wick while noticing Bernard's look. She smiles at her husband, and she holds his glance a few seconds. The tavern closes when the singing stops. Zees knows her husband will no longer be in the mood when the singing stops.

"Father Thomas, what do you think about America?" Jacob asks. "Do you believe the stories about free land ...

more land than one man can plow? What about the oil —
do you believe they have found oil in Kansas? Would you
sell? Would you leave Solotoye?"

"I don't know what to believe. The railroad pamphlets
are printed to sell land. I don't know if I would believe
what they say. But letters from friends and family, why
would they lie? They wouldn't lie."

My father listens intently and nods. Bernard and Wolf
don't speak. "If I could get permission to sell my property,
and I had enough money for the voyage and enough to buy
land, I think … I think I would go. We have no control
Father — no control over our lives. The Kontor tells us
what we can and cannot do, when to get up in the morning, when to go to bed at night, when to eat, when to shi
… Sorry Father."

"Yes, that's true, but will it be any different there? If
you don't know where you're going, it's best to stay where
you are." Father Thomas turns to his left catching a glimpse
of Commissar Shishkin in conversation with Herr Buchs.
Hoping Shishkin heard his encouragement for the men to
stay in Solotoye, Father Thomas returns, disappointed, to
hear more of Jacob's views on leaving.

"… but when it gets so bad where you are, sometimes
you have to leave even if you don't know where you're
going. Maybe you just hope it will be better, or at least …
I don't know," grumbled Jacob as he motioned for Wolf to
fill his glass.

"You know Father Thomas, I get more customers than you. The men obviously prefer my stories to those you pull out of that book of yours," teased Push.

"How dare you compare your pitiful peasant parables to the Bible, to the word of God," replied the young priest trying to control his emotions. He slyly removed his paper from the table, placing it by his side on the bench, hiding it from the men.

Jacob, Bernard, and Wolf listened and watched the verbal combatants not indicating support for either. They had heard much of this argument many times. Zees shook her head and rolled her eyes at her father as she walked by. Stay sat impatiently on Jacob's table waiting for Push to pick him up. Stay forcefully pawed the air letting Push know he needed attention.

"Well, Wiggens, at least one poor creature will listen to your tiresome tavern-tales. I'll bet you pay him quite well. Am I right Wiggens?" The men burst into laughter. Push swept up his cat and retreated.

Monsters and Milking Stools

Was I the only one afraid of those badgering beasts with tough skin made of brown boards? As a young girl, they frightened me. Monsters from the steppe sneak into the village at night to scare the children. Giant arms extend, move violently in a circular motion, and bellow a foreign and metered language — whoosh … whoosh …whoosh. From my backyard, with Father close to protect against a monstrous charge, I stood on a milking stool and threw rocks over our broken birch-fence to scare them away.

> Over broken birch-fence,
> Rocks fall short.
> Monsters remain. They stand tall.
> Stool gives way. I fall.

I outgrew the stool, and I stopped throwing stones. On a warm and windy summer night, four creatures crawled from cocoons and turned into beautiful brown butterflies — wooden butterflies.

On my sixteenth birthday, I jumped over the fence and apologized for my warlike behavior. I embraced friendly windmills that look like wooden butterflies.

Sweep . Clean . Polish

Is it peculiar that we sweep a dirt farmyard with a straw broom? We sweep dirt from our houses. We polish the wooden floors. We polish the kettles in the kitchen. We dust the windowsills and so much more. That makes sense. We sweep. We clean. We polish. Sweep, clean, and polish. We hang up Grandpa's hat. Why would I question that? I didn't. Why would I question sweeping a dirt farmyard? I didn't, until ... rowdy Russian boys made fun of me.

What were they doing in Solotoye?
What were they doing on my street?
I stared wildly as they mocked my
Chore and naked exposed feet.

Can I stop the returning image
And embarrassment of that day,
As I sweep earthen floors
With a whisk made of hay?

Jeering echoes, broom, dirt,
Absent shoes —
Choose to remember —
I lose.

Spiele' Gehen
Benches and Flowers Say Welcome

Visiting we go.

Simple wooden benches sit next to happy houses, against warm walls, facing silent streets. Countless rough bottoms buff the bench tops smooth.

Small, well-attended, fragrant flower-gardens border house and benches.

Welcome. They say.
Come. Sit. Tell me your news.
Tell me a story.
Recount your day.

We have tobacco. We have drink.
Come. Tell me what you think.

When glasses are empty,
And we are tired of song,
We will watch the sunset,
And forget all that is wrong.

Family Dinner

"Mother, thank you for inviting us to Sunday dinner. I get my favorite meal, and I didn't have to cook. It's not my birthday, is it? Anton, would you help Bernard and Wolf with the extra table and benches. Mother, what can I do?"

"Everything is ready. Just need the table and benches brought in and set. I thought we could put white sheets over the tables — make it look ... nice."

"Well, I can put the dishes out." I moved close to Mother and whispered in her ear, "Why? You never invite people to dinner ... and Push too?"

"I don't know. We might not be here. I wanted to ... Push is family."

"Father, I've written another poem. I think you'll like it."

"What's it about?"

"Time — how time becomes friend and enemy, giver and taker." Father scratched his head with a puzzled look. "You know, how time gives us wisdom, and how it steals our youth. It's not finished. Maybe you can help me with it? You always have many things to say."

"Emma, have you talked to Greta lately?" asked Wolf.

"No, Wolf, haven't seen her in years."

"Always have to make jokes. You should try making them funny," Wolf retorted.

"I talked to her yesterday while doing laundry. She said to tell you that she loves you like ... like the bear loves honey, and she can't live without her honey."

"Now that's funny," Bernard quipped. Everybody laughed, except Wolf of course. He thought I was serious.

"Enough," scolded Mother. "It's time to eat."

We pushed and squeezed into our places. Father sat at the head of the table and gave thanks. We listened with bowed heads. A furtive glance at Father told me this was going to take awhile. A veiled rolling of my head eased my already strained neck. Father has a tendency to ramble when it comes to prayers he can create. He ended this embellished benediction with an extended thanks to Push for bringing vodka.

I thanked God for Father's overdue, "Amen."

I nodded my head emphatically as I repeated, "AMEN." I received a questioning glance from Father and Mother. Bernard tossed me a knowing smile and nod.

"Push, what are you doing at the children's table?" asked Father.

"Walter, Helga, Peter, and Maria said they had stories they wanted to tell me, so ..."

"Eat everyone. There's more food on the stove," commanded Mother.

As we ate, Zees, Bernard, Wolf, Father, and Mother said little. The children chattered with Push about this and that, and I kept conversation going trying to engage everyone. It wasn't easy, but Anton likes to talk. He enjoyed telling everyone about his new tools. The length of that conversation certainly exceeded my interest in it — something about a plane, hammer. I don't know. The other men appeared happy that they didn't have to talk.

"The men clean up," I bellowed with mother-like authority. "It's my birthday wish."

"What? Your birthday isn't 'till ... oh shit, I forgot her birthday again," said Anton. The men and children laughed. The women shook their heads.

"Fine. Go smoke your pipes and have a drink," I replied.

"No," said Mother. "I say we sit here, and we enjoy Push's vodka. Wolf, get the glasses. Bernard, get the vodka. Bitte."

And so, we sat at the tables with dirty dishes everywhere. Push squeezed next to me. We toasted many things — Solotoye, good health, good crops, more rain, less heat and wind ... Anton's plane or hammer.

I watched Wolf enjoying himself. He's twenty years old now. He's already twenty, but he's only twenty. He's an adult, but not. He's mature, but not. He noticed me staring. Wolf responded with a quizzical look and an awkward head-gesture.

"Emma!"

"Oh, sorry. To ..."

"To the children." Push made the toast, 'Here's to making life better for the children.' "Better for the children," Anton repeated.

I raised my glass. "Better for the children," I said as I downed what little remained of my drink. I looked for the children. They were playing on the beds.

Can we really make life better for our children? We have to leave Solotoye, I told myself as I watched them toss large feather pillows at each other. Maria's mischievous laughter caught my attention as she willingly got hit in the face by many pillows. "Better for the children?" I mumbled.

My thoughts returned to my younger brother, to Greta, and to their future children, if they marry. His eyes sparkle, and he becomes animated when he talks about America. He needs the dream. If we get there, I'm sure he'll make a success of whatever he does. He wants more than Solotoye can give. Greta sees Wolf the same way. She sees a good father for her children.

"Push, what about the tavern?" I asked. "What will the men do?"

"Till tomorrow they must wait ... a closed sign's on the gate," he replied with sleepy eyes and slurred words.

I struggled to raise my empty glass and smiled my acknowledgement of his rhyming response. He's a natural storyteller, I thought.

Closed — the word bothered me. We won't have Wiggens' Place anymore. I should stop drinking. The toasting ended followed by an awkward silence. Father noticed the somber mood, so he burst into a sloppy rendition of *My Solotoye*.

Who will clean this mess? Doesn't matter, I told myself.

Together, stay together, I thought as familiar, happy lyrics filled the room.

Rolling Thunder

Change — it comes. I sense it.

Rumblings about brave, adventurous souls that left Solotoye years past persist like latent ambers in evening's fire. Rolling thunder moves fast on the steppe heading for our quiet village. There's no stopping it.

I know little of this place called Kansas. A bewildering feeling that our future lies there envelopes me like heavy fog lays on bottom land.

I sense it. Don't want to stop it. Want to make it happen — to lead our families to America.

America, where there is
More land than one can till,
Ample grains, a small purse to fill.
Men and women are free —
Women — much more to be.

Bring dark clouds — bring stormy weather — bring the spark that lights the fire of change.

Rolling thunder.

Skirts . Yokes . Buckets

Solotoye tenders a good morning. A warming sun hangs above the eastern horizon like a large pearl hiding behind pale-gray morning mist. Young women casually draw water from deep, cool wells. Some make their way home with yokes on shoulders, buckets hanging, moving gracefully along rutted, dusty streets. Skirts sway to the fluid, sensual motion of their hips drawing the attention of boys and men. Water rarely spills. Men and boys never notice when it does.

Greta and I take our time allowing others to go before us. I know Greta needs to talk about Wolf, and I have important things to tell her. She won't like what I have to say. I search her face and eyes with concern.

"Greta, I have something to tell you." I pause, staring at her.

"What?"

"Last night, when Father, Bernard, and Wolf came home from the tavern, Mother heard them talking about America … about Kansas. Father thinks the time has come to leave Solotoye."

"What does this mean? What about you … Anton … Bernard, and Zees? What will they do? What does your Mother think?"

"I don't know Greta. Maybe Father is just talking again. You know how he gets when he drinks too much.

Mother will do what Father wants."

"Yes, but … if your father does decide to leave, Wolf will go with him. Maybe he wants to go … maybe he doesn't want a wife … perhaps … what will you and Anton do?"

"I don't know. Anton talks about leaving. We talk. We argue. Everyone talks about it Greta. Not many leave — not since those families twenty … thirty years ago."

"I can't leave my family Emma. At times, I want to leave Solotoye. Sometimes, I feel I don't belong here, but I can't leave my family. My father will never leave Solotoye. I love Wolf, and I … the water. Mother waits for the ..."

"Greta, stop." I pulled her hand from the yoke.

"I should go."

"Wait. We need to talk." She gave me a look of resignation. "Greta, I have this feeling that our destined path — yours, mine, Zees' — leads us there. I don't know when or how, but it will happen. We need to prepare ourselves."

"Emma, stop. Prepare all you want, but don't drag others into your scheme … dream, whatever you call it. Of course, you think it a good idea. Your family wants to go. My family will stay. Do you understand?"

"I do understand, but you have Wolf to think about. Right?" She gave me a questioning look. "Greta, I really think my family will go. You said you don't belong here, and that you want to leave. Well … you want Wolf to marry you, and …"

"I can't think about that now."

"Greta, what about your children? Do you want to raise a family here? And what about the way they treat women here? Men act differently towards women in America."

"You don't know that's true. Do you?"

"No, I don't." I didn't know what to say. I looked away. I studied girls and young women, under yoke, as they labored up the street. Silence. I continued to observe the yokes and buckets. "Greta, look at them."

"Look at whom?"

"Them! Us! We carry water every day. I don't mind doing it, but ... It symbolizes ..."

"It what?"

"The yoke, the weight of it, the daily obligation, ... the yoke — it holds women down. Don't you see?" She shook her head bewildered.

"I don't understand Emma."

"I'm not sure. This scene, something in Solotoye, makes my skin itch. We stumble through too many days now. Don't you feel that way Greta?"

"I agree life could be better in Solotoye, but I don't have solutions Emma. What I believe ... the one thing I do know ... I should take care of myself. I must survive this place, this time. Then I need to find a way to do this with Wolf in my life. That's all ... all I can handle now. I don't have time to understand your ... symbol. I only have time to live my life. Carrying water from the wells, cooking, cleaning … laundry … spinning — the elders expect it. They demand it. I do it because …"

"What if Wolf doesn't marry you?"

"I'll survive Emma. You, Zees, Anton, Bernard … all the Zimmer family will be in America. And I will be here with my family."

Greta lifted the yoke to her shoulders and moved up the road — leaving a trail of water.

Harvest Festival and Church Picnic

Beautiful September weather
Solotoye together

Food, drink, song, and dance
Time to give the boy another glance

A good time
A happy time

Games needing skill, others mostly luck
Celebrate our hard work

Father gives a blessing
Things at the river I won't be confessing

A good time
A happy time

Beautiful September weather
Solotoye together

The Cove

"Wolf, I have good news," said Bernard raising his eyebrows and showing a devilish grin. "This comes from a reliable source."

"Well, what … tell me. What can be so good about this news? Did you get me out of digging the nushnik? That would be good news."

"No, much better than that," replied Bernard still with a mischievous smile. "Zees mentioned that Greta, Elka, and Katherina were going to the cove today, and you know what that means …"

"This better be true Bernard."

"I don't lie, but if you think I do, well … you should stay here. An early start on the new shitter would please Father."

"When are they going? Are they going to their usual place?"

"Yes, they plan to meet at the wells around two. I'll tell Father you went to the plant."

Wolf rushes to the gate knowing he has little time. They — Klaus, Walter, and Wolf — must time their approach perfectly.

Wolf spends solitary time prowling the trails up and down Matushka's left bank. He likes being unattached. Most of the time, he prefers it. Like a wolf tracks its prey, he stalks space ... to be alone ... to think. His territory includes the river, much of the steppe, and the village. Strength, confidence, and agility dominate his traits. He intimidates other males without effort, without knowing. Females find his power and independence irresistible. Today, he travels with a pack.

Like veins on an old man's hand, paths from the village to the river pulse with activity, though slowly and irregularly. They cross. They merge. They end unexpectedly, and run parallel to each other. Some become conspicuous while others fade into surrounding brush. When not used regularly, they become constricted and nature reclaims them. Those still being used on a regular basis end in the same place — a sandy cove used for bathing, laundry, and swimming.

The canine-like suitors approach the area slowly, so they won't be seen or heard. They timed the catch perfectly. The girls arrived. They started to undress. The young men relish this initial phase. They savor walking up to water's edge, pretending to go for a swim, trying to catch a closer look. Wolf, although never discussed with Klaus or Walter, prefers to watch Greta shake out her hair. He loves the way it falls down her back just above her narrow waist.

Greta busies herself chatting with Elka and Katherina as she slips from her long gray skirt and unbuttons her shirt. She lets the shirt slide off her shoulders and fall to the ground. Her sleeveless sarpinka under-garment floats over her body. Greta slowly pushes the top off each shoulder and steps out of the light cotton-cover. Wolf stares as Greta runs her hands through auburn hair, shaking her head from side to side, trying to separate the long strands.

Afternoon sun spreads a golden light on the sandy beach and on the girls' cascading hair and naked backs. Their skin pales like the birch under the sun's rays.

Motionless and speechless, the men don't blink for fear of missing something. They observe the girls entering the water. They contemplate the timing of their next move. Not yet, they decide without speaking or looking at each other.

The girls acclimate themselves to the water. Washcloths and small bars of homemade soap move over bodies to the amusement of the voyeurs in the nearby cottonwoods.

Walter nudges Wolf whispering a pleading, "Now?"

Wolf anxiously nods, and the three move from their cover towards the beach.

"Remember, we're going swimming. Maybe they will ask us to join them," whispers Wolf as they enjoy a muffled laugh. They make their long-awaited approach.

Elka and Katherina scream, "GET OUT, LEAVE … NOW," as they dip into the water leaving only shoulders and heads exposed. Greta turns and faces the intruders. Her eyes engage Wolf's. She smiles and continues bathing. Their eye contact becomes intense.

"What are you doing here? Leave. Please leave," Elka

begs.

Greta and Wolf remain locked in eye contact not hearing or seeing anyone or anything.

"What are you doing here?" Greta asks Wolf.

"Ah … swimming … we're going swimming."

Greta smiles, moves the cloth over soapy shoulders, cups water, and lets it run down her chest and back. Greta watches Wolf's eyes follow the torpid movements of her hands and loitering beads of water.

"Well, why wait?" asks Greta. "We don't mind, do we girls?" Elka and Katherina stare at Greta, puzzled. "It's only fair. Take off your clothes. We want to see those … muscles." The girls have a good laugh becoming comfortable with the situation. But they secretly hope the prowlers won't accept the offer Greta has recklessly made.

"Ah … well … er," mumbles Wolf as he looks to Klaus and Walter for help. "Maybe we should find a different place." He stumbles backwards.

Greta and Wolf make eye contact again. They both willingly display playful smiles on their sun-drenched faces.

"Greta, will you meet me at the wells tonight?" asks Wolf drawing on his natural confidence.

"Why? I'm not going swimming with you," she replies smiling.

"Oh, no. Just … want to talk. At nine?"

Greta gives him a flirtatious smile. "Wells at nine," she

affirms.

The sated pack turns and trots towards the village.

Greta flashes a hopeful smile at Elka and Katherina.

Die Brautdusch

Heavy boots, dusty shoes, and small, happy feet
Pound wooden planks at Hochzeit.
Weathered hands slap thighs to the
Dulcimer's twangy beat.

It all seems to fit —
Accordion and violin push the tempo
Faster and faster
Until Grandpa is forced to sit.

Many songs fill the crowded room.
On this wedding day —
A special one for
The bride and groom.

Father's favorite song —
Most men sing along.

Men sing to the young couple
On their wedding day.
Husband and wife listen carefully —
The words have much to say.

Die Brautdusch.

Mayor Mary Wade

"Zees, Greta, look at this photograph." Zees tried in vain to steady the paper in my trembling hands. "What a place! We must go ... what a place! What a ..."

"What do you mean, what a place?" asked Greta looking at the photograph. "Why do you have a picture of these women?"

"I got the photograph from Marta. It came in a letter several years ago from her uncle in Kansas — in Ellis." I had difficulty saying the names of these unfamiliar places. "These women, well ... they make laws like the Kontor, the soviet. The village voted for them. They voted to make the women their government. Look at this lady. Marta said she's called *Mayor — Mayor Mary Wade*. She has a position like Commissar Shishkin. Can you believe it? These women rule the men. They tell the men what to do. I'm going. I don't care what Anton says. I'm going."

"Look at their dresses and their hair," said Greta as she snatched the paper from Zees. "I want to look like that, only younger. Do you think all women in this village dress this way?"

"Do you know what these women did ... what they did for their village? They closed the taverns ... the drinking places. The men have guns that they shoot in the taverns. You know — when drunk. So, the women made them close the taverns ... to stop the shooting. Can you believe that? And they give land to anyone who wants it. That's quite something — a village where women make the rules." I shook my head in disbelief.

"That can never happen here Emma," said Zees. "I don't want you closing Father's tavern. What will he do? What will I do?" Zees forced a laugh while looking at Greta and me. "How do we know we would make better laws than the men?"

I gave Zees a look of disbelief. "They would certainly be better for women, wouldn't they? That's good enough for me."

"Well, just so you don't close Wiggens' Place."

"I'll leave Wiggens' Place open. But I'll make a new law requiring a tavern just for women." Zees let out a small chuckle. The photograph represented hope for women — for us. Our eyes remained on the dresses.

Greta would not like what I needed to say, but I knew we could work things out, so the three of us would always be together. I looked at Greta and spoke to Zees. "If Father leaves, will you and Bernard go too?" Greta's face changed. It flushed with fear.

"Yes, Bernard wants to go. Our struggles pile up like manure back by the fence. Sorry, that's not a good example. He dreams day and night of our lives there. And, Father will go with us."

"What does Wolf think," I asked? Greta didn't want to hear Zees' answer.

"He wants to go, of course. He wants to create a new life in a new place. He talks about making his fortune in Kansas. He rambles on about cheap land, cattle, and oil — always about finding oil on his land. But he wants to come back to Solotoye. Coming back doesn't make sense. Does it?" We ignored the troubling question.

"Zees, I must convince Anton to go. If we help each other get started, we'll do well. Unused land in Kansas waits for us. We need to persuade Wolf to marry Greta."

"I don't want to marry Wolf if that means I must leave my family."

"But you love him." Greta looked at me with moist eyes. She nodded.

"I do."

"Maybe your father will change his mind if you marry Wolf."

"No, he won't. You don't understand Emma. I don't want to leave, but ..."

"Greta, we should stay together. If one goes, we all go."

"Emma, that sounds nice, but ... life doesn't work that way."

She was right. I wanted her to be wrong. "Greta, are you saying that if Wolf asks to marry you and wants to leave, that you will say no?" She hung her head and stared at the ground. After a prolonged silence, she looked at me.

"Yes ... I think I would say no. I think I would ... I don't know. It would be nice if we stayed together. I would like that. I don't want to think about this anymore ... today."

Sleeves Like Cotton Clouds

I don't remember exactly when I lost my senses — maybe Monday morning. I really don't remember. It doesn't matter. I lost my senses over Mayor Mary Wade. I didn't care. I wanted to be like her. I copied her hairstyle. I tried standing erect like her with my head slightly tilted back. I practiced pulling my hair up with a small knot at the top of my head. I stood at the stove with my nose slightly in the air. Anton, Peter, and Maria laughed and wanted to know if my neck bothered me. Anton's parents shook their heads secretly hoping this … thing passed quickly.

I studied the photograph of Mayor Mary Wade and the council of women. The old and faded picture made it difficult to discern the pattern of Mary's dress. Crazed and demented … I proceeded.

Two houses west of the Wasen House lives Old Frau Hessen, our reclusive seamstress. She lives with two goats — one named Gella and one called Gita — a black mother cat Frau Hessen calls Schwartz Matushka — sometimes Schwartzie — and a sewing machine the color of Schwartzie.

The black scary machine sits next to Frau Hessen's dining table. Unfinished work covers table and benches. Schwartzie lays on top of the soft cloth. The grumpy and peculiar seamstress reluctantly showed me how to make the needle go up and down by moving the big flat pedal down by the floor. She showed me how to push the material under the needle, and she warned me to watch my fingers. When I showed the photograph to Frau Hessen, she shook her head. I think I heard her, or Schwartzie, or both, hiss. After more begging, Frau Hessen finally agreed to let me use her black machine. She refused when I asked her to help make the dress.

After days of pleading, Anton gave me money for material. My wonderful and naive husband thought it would turn out … good enough to wear. He thought I wouldn't waste the money. Maybe he didn't think these things at all. Perhaps he simply wanted me to stop pestering him about the dress.

I did it! I thanked Frau Hessen, gathered up my dress, and backed out of the crowded workroom bumping into Gita. I excused myself and smiled apologetically to the frowning old seamstress. I closed the door behind me and yelled, "I did it!"

On the way home, I imagined that a special dress like this should be worn to a wedding or to church — sitting proudly in the front row. So, I wore my Mayor Mary dress the following Sunday. Anton and his parents quickly made excuses to stay at home when I carefully stepped into the kitchen showing off the dress.

Peter and Maria escorted me to church. A bothersome breeze tugged at faulty basting. Instinctively, we quickened our pace. I held onto both sleeves at the shoulders. Elbows clasped loose material to my sides. I leaned into the breeze. "Jesus," I muttered. Peter dashed here and there picking up cloth with undone clinging thread.

I noticed the hem of my skirt also coming undone and dragging in the dirt. The neck quietly choked me. Somewhere in the waistband, I must have left a needle because I kept getting a sharp sticking pain as my left foot hit the ground. I tried limping. It helped. When I dragged my left foot, the pain subsided. Peter and Maria thought they should mimic their mother. Three children — two small, one large — hobbled down the street. We left three intermittent and scraggly lines in the dirt as we moved entertainingly along. Neighbors stopped and stared with bewildered faces.

Why did I do it? My poor children!

We made it into church — Peter and Maria still dragging one foot. The loud scraping echo caused heads to turn. We quickly sat on a bench behind the women and children. Hands covered mouths. I heard gasps. Peter stuffed more material into his already bulging pockets. I wondered if I could make it home without the whole dress falling around my ankles. Perhaps the breeze will have pity on me.

My hair screamed — pleading for its release from the too tight bun. The corners of my eyes stretched wide like I was in a frozen state of surprise. Blinking became a chore, eyes started to water. Peter pulled a piece of material from his pocket and handed it to me. How can he be so brave and caring at a time like this?

My beautiful sleeves — they looked nothing like ... their dresses. Big puffy sleeves looked like cotton clouds — the right noticeably bigger than the left. I don't know how that happened. I wanted to puff up the left with my hand, but touching it could cause more damage.

"OUCH!"

The needle hidden in my waistband jabbed me again. I pulled up what was left of my jacket, and I rolled the waist over. Found it! Tangled black thread hung from a sharp shiny needle.

As Peter and I inspected the bloodstained object, I sensed people staring, so I sheepishly looked up. Father Thomas and others glared. I held up the needle and thread, waved, and forced a smile while wiping away more tears. Peter and Maria mimicked their crazed mother waving to gawking faces.

Peter carefully took the needle from my hand and whispered, "Mother, are you two whiskers away?"

I lowered my head. Face-to-face with my son, I asked, "What? Where did you learn that?"

"From you Mother," Peter replied a little too loudly. "You say it all the time."

I smiled at Peter, ruffled his hair, and replied quietly, "Yes, definitely two whiskers away." I wiped my eyes again. For a moment, I thought I could see better this way. I touched my scalp gently with bandaged fingertip. Pain.

The following thoughts raced through my aching head. Please don't let my hair fall out. How am I going to kneel? Perhaps we should leave now?

I must look ridiculous. I will never do such a stupid thing again. Make a promise. But I knew it was useless.

Leaving church, Maria asked, "Mother, can we do the funny walk again?"

I went to see Marta early Monday morning. Having been in church, she asked if I wanted to borrow some thread. She couldn't stop smiling as we talked. I pretended not to notice. I asked if I could write to her uncle in Ellis. I wanted more information on the council of women. With a titter, Marta suggested I ask Mary for her dress. Studying my bandaged fingertips, Marta decided it best to address the envelope. Leaving Marta's house, I noticed her in the doorway shaking her head.

"Why do people keep doing that?"

Roads Here and There

Like a lazy letter 'T' lying on its back with arms stretching to its sides, Little Karman Road and River Road meet in the middle of Solotoye at the south end of the village square. Little Karman enters the village from the east, squeezing between, and dodging whooshing wings of two wooden butterflies to the south and the same number to the north. River Road parallels the wandering flow of Matushka Volga's watery pathway.

Solotoye's roads become dusty and rutted in good weather—impassable in bad. The roads consist of nothing more than wagon tracks taking us here and there ... never far. We trade wagons for sleighs when winter freezes the ground and packs the snow solid. Tiny bells tingle. They jingle as playful horses prance along the winter landscape. They jingle and tingle as horses pull simple homemade-sleighs carrying all sizes of smiling, rose-colored faces bundled in woolen blankets.

Rocks Plunk Plunk

Day's closing — eventide — I rest and meditate at Matushka's sanctuary. My eyes scan from north to west across the river's drowsy drift. I gaze beyond hills and forest. Soothing soft tones reach into the vast evening sky. I seize the twilight like tenuous paper takes possession of the artist's water colors. A beautiful pale-blue horizon hides the sun. Scattered delicate clouds, like a child's hand, catch rays and let them escape through playful fingers. Elusive silver streams of sunlight appear free and mysterious. I envy them. Matushka paints the scene with fluid strokes. I breathe it. I invite the colors to enter my sacred room on this tree-lined rocky shore.

I watch Peter and Maria trying to skip rocks on river's flat palette. Rocks go plunk. Children laugh and silently seek Mother's admiration. My beautiful children complete this lovely landscape — this magical moment.

To my right, three pines lean over the water's seductive surface as if drinking, or testing the water for a swim. A mile beyond, Matushka bends slightly to the east and disappears. Down-river, Matushka runs wide and straight until her banks appear to meet. Tree-covered hills across the river always invite, but they are a restricted area.

Plunk, plunk. I return their infectious smiles and nod. Tiny white feet play with gentle waves that soak the sandy cove. Catfish jump and slap the surface with agile tails as if to mimic Peter and Maria. Plunk, plunk, whap, whap, plunk ... whap. Pale-blue light reluctantly gives way to shades of blue and purple. It all saturates my soul.

Imagination. I purchase a ticket to go beyond my boundaries, span Matushka's moat, level this impassible forested range, and to breach a fresh vista of the west. Silence ... space ... freedom. I smile.

An eager and naive face presses the cool window as the locomotive pulls a solitary passenger into Ellis. All the town's people come to welcome their new mayor. I open the window, wave warmly, enthusiastically, and smile. It could happen. Ellis. I belong there.

"Peter, stop teasing your sister."

The return trip lasted a moment. I disembark. Confined space and restrained freedoms welcome me home. Silence ... a deep and prolonged sigh of resignation slips away.

"Peter, Maria, we must go."

Anton worries when we are gone too long. Mother Wasen angers. Change my world. Change my life ... change for Anton, Peter, and Maria ... for me.

As we walk hand-in-hand leaving our sanctuary, I whisper, "Change — create the spark — kindle the fire."

Peter and Maria look up at their mother and smile.

Small trusting hands — a beautiful day's closing.

Log House With Thatched Roof

"Are you leaking?" I smiled devilishly at Push, who was perched perilously on his grass roof. His half-glance and slight tilt of his head spoke a playful admonishment. "Well, you know what I mean ... the roof, is the roof leaking?"

"No, Emma, just adding more straw in places where the roof is a little bare."

"Need some help?"

"Almost finished." Push gave me a look that asked why I was there.

"I came by to talk," I said anticipating his question.

"You came to the right person and the right place for that. What do you want to talk about?"

"Anything."

"Anything? Lets see ... how about the cost of a barrel of Zig? No?"

"How about ... your red hat. I remember your hat as a little girl. Where did you find it? I don't know any markets that sell red hats."

"I bought a light-brown ... like everyone else. But I wanted something different. I get tired of black, gray, and brown. So, I dyed it. Actually, my wife did."

"I like it Push. Let me hold the ladder while you come down."

"Danke."

"Where's Stay?"

"Haven't seen him since breakfast. Want to sit at the tables?"

"How about the steps ... in the sun? The warm rays feel good this time of year."

"Right. Did you know that this might be the oldest house in Solotoye?"

"I know three log houses with thatched roofs remain, and the colonists built all the houses this way. Did the Wiggens family build it?"

"No, my great, great grandfather bought it. It's close to one hundred thirty years old. It takes a lot of time to repair. Wouldn't have it any other way though."

"I understand. I don't like the newer homes with the tin roofs and flat boards, like our house, the Wasen house. I do like the different colors of the weathered tin. Rain beats the tin like a drum, but it doesn't rain that often, does it? Hail on tin roofs scares the children and older girls acting like they're six." I noticed a weak smile.

"I barely hear rain or hail. The grass cushions the impact. The thickness of the logs and thatch keeps the house cool in summer and warm in winter. We lost some log houses to fire. They tore down others for the lumber. I miss them."

I nudged Push with my elbow. "Will Matushka flood this spring?"

"Depends on the snow up river and along the rivers

that drain into Matushka. Snowed little this winter. Don't know about anyplace else. Not likely it would reach Solotoye if it did flood. Doesn't happen all that often — that it gets close to our village."

"Any Kontor or Shishkin stories? Remember when Zees, Greta, and I broke into their office? I can't believe Greta made us do it. She always gets people into trouble. See, I made you laugh. We don't laugh enough. Let's make a rule — a good hearty laugh each day, not just a giggle or a chuckle, not one of those stupid Kontor rules, but our rule."

"Why did you break into their office?"

"Rules — we made a list of rules for the Kontor. It was Greta's idea."

"Right."

"We figured if the Kontor makes rules for how we live our lives, we should make some rules for them. Makes sense. Don't you think?"

"So, what rules did you have on the list?"

"Silly stuff — no sneezing on Tuesdays ... if caught, public whipping — and no polishing boots after sundown. I thought of that one. Did you know a village in Kansas allows women to make and enforce the rules? Ellis ... they call it Ellis."

"Yes, Zees told me. What's her name, the mayor?"

"I call her Mayor Mary. If we go, I should become mayor."

"Emma Wasen as mayor — sounds dangerous," laughed Push.

"See, doesn't it feel good to laugh?"

"Ya. Ya. You do have that affect on people Emma Wasen. That should get you elected mayor."

Stay squeezed through the gate sauntering down the boardwalk with bushy tail in the air.

"I should go. Mother Wasen searches the streets for me when I'm gone too long."

"Come back anytime Emma … I mean Mayor Wasen. I need the laughs."

"Bye Push. Bye Stay." I turned, pointed my finger at the cat, and commanded, "STAY."

Push chuckled, then burst into laughter as he waved goodbye shaking his head. I peeked up and down the street before opening the gate.

"Mother Wasen, come out wherever you are," I joked quietly to myself.

Herr Baumann's Pig

Solotoye boasts about its love, friendliness, about its beauty. Like the steppe's spring bounty of tulips and blue-bells mixed with heather grass, sometimes the beautiful relationships appear peculiar. The more than friendly interest of Herr Baumann's portly pig and Herr Reisling's raucous rooster puzzle the people of Solotoye. Affectionately, we call her Baumann's Beauty or BeeBee. Respectfully, we call him Reisling's Rooster.

As with most village animals, this pair of poultry and pork roam the streets freely. Like a king, Reisling's Rooster struts, scratches, and crows his way through the day, claiming the whole village as his kingdom. BeeBee follows him tirelessly, lovingly, telling him she adores his red crown. She applauds his pecking prowess, and she marvels at the melody of his constant crowing. Reisling's Rooster loves the attention. Although too proud to say it, he loves Bee-Bee.

They spend long days together. They reluctantly part when church bells signal dinner. Baumann's Beauty sighs a parting grunt. She bids the bird good night as her poultry partner retreats to his farmyard. BeeBee finds her gate. When Herr Baumann forgets to open it, she rarely minds the wait. She will dine and rest — at dawn she must look her best.

The Storyteller

"Herr Wiggens, will you tell us the story of *Push, Pull, and Stay*? begged Peter resting anxiously on the step below Push. His friends echoed the request wanting to hear the old and funny story — a favorite of the children along with *Ivan the River Bandit*.

"Do you mean how I received my name — how my cat and horse got their names?" asked Push.

"Yes, the story of the wagon on River Road."

"Very well. I enjoy telling the story to such beautiful children," Push replied as he adjusted his seating.

Push cleared his throat and began the story.

"Once upon a time, a very handsome strong man lived with a very smart horse and a very lazy cat. The cat always wore a red hat …"

"NO, NO, NO, Herr Wiggens, the cat doesn't wear a red hat," the children interrupted while laughing.

"Oh yes, I forgot. The cat always wore a green …"

"NO! The cat doesn't wear a hat. Remember?"

"Right. I remember now. The man in the red hat lived with a very smart horse and a lazy cat. The cat never wore a hat. It didn't even own a hat. An old wagon, made from the finest wood, lived in the handsome man's shed. The wagon complained about everything — how the wind and rain ruined its beautiful wood, how too much sun stole its rich color, but mostly it complained about the ruts in River

Road. It moaned and cried constantly, 'Stop, my feet can't take this anymore...'"

"Herr Wiggens, wagons roll on wheels, not feet," corrected the little girl sitting next to Push.

"Right, of course you're right," acknowledged Push smiling at the attentive group. "But why do wagons have wheels and not feet?"

"Because wagons need wheels. People need feet," offered a shy boy sitting to Push's right.

"Very good, Hans. Are there any other reasons why wagons don't have feet?"

"They roll. People walk ... sometimes we run, but rolling is faster than walking and running ... well, we get tired from running. Wagons don't get tired."

"Right, Julia," agreed Push as he patted her head.

"One spring day when the last snow melted, the wagon's wheels stuck in the road's muddy low-spot. The man in the red hat crawled down from the wagon as the horse studied the situation carefully. The cat, of course, slept. The handsome man scratched his head in a puzzled way. His thoughts became muddled. 'Push. You must push my backside,' suggested the wagon." The children smiled knowingly. "And so, the man in the red hat pushed and pushed. The man pushed, the horse pulled, the wagon roared, and the cat snored."

Rowdy laughter erupted from the children. The boys displayed the antics of ... young boys. Push, pleased with the children's response, smiled, waited for the boys to settle down, and continued.

"Well, the strong man pushed and the horse pulled until the wagon slipped out of the mud. The horse stopped and the man in the red hat returned to the wagon seat. The horse glanced at the man in the red hat shaking its head in disbelief. The wagon chuckled. The horse pointed with its head towards the low spot. Two muddy boots, trapped in the mire, cried for help."

The children relished this part of the story. One of the boys laughed so hard he doubled over, lost his balance, and rolled down one step. This, of course, caused the others to laugh even harder.

"Wait, the boots escape from their muddy jail. They squirmed, struggled, and finally popped free, shaking themselves off like two dogs after a swim. They ran frantically to the wagon and jumped in. Big cold toes peaked from holes in the man's socks. The frenzied toes wiggled signaling the man to return their warm cover. The horse faced the hill and guided the funny foursome home to Solotoye. And they lived happily ever ...."

"NO, NO, Herr Wiggens," the children corrected him again. "What about the hawk? You forgot about the hawk."

"Oh yes ... a hawk enters the story. I forget that part every time," said Herr Wiggens as the children glanced at each other knowing what came next in the story.

"From that day on, a funny thing happened on their trips along River Road. Every time they approached that low spot, the horse would pause and wait for the man in the red hat to push the wagon. Before the man in the red hat stepped down from the wagon, he would tell the cat to stay. The cat, surprisingly, did obey. After pushing for a short distance, the horse stopped and allowed the man in the red hat to return to the wagon seat and his lazy cat.

"The man in the red hat didn't know a red-tailed hawk always soared high above studying their ridiculous behavior. One sunny day, the hawk swooped down and landed in a cottonwood tree next to the road. 'My friends call me Hawk,' she said. 'What names do you go by?' The man in the red hat introduced everyone. Hawk replied, 'Your conduct on River Road is very peculiar. You need names that reflect your silly antics. I christen you *Push*, the horse *Pull*, the cat *Stay*, and the wagon, hmmm, well, just *Wagon*.'"

"Pull liked her new name. Stay answered to his new name knowing food and scratching usually followed. Wagon complained, but nobody listened. And the man in the red hat, well, that's how the man in the red hat became known as Push. And so, the horse named Pull, the cat christened Stay, the man called Push, and the wagon with the funny name Wagon, lived happily ever after."

The children looked at each other waiting for someone to say it. They always ended the story the same way. "You are that handsome man in the red hat, right?"

"Right, I'm the very handsome and strong man in the red hat," Push replied as he smiled sheepishly. "Next time, shall I tell you the story of *Ivan the River Bandit*?"

"Yes, the river bandit story!"

"I must return home. Pull and Stay worry when I *stay* too long." Push emphasized the word for affect. "Wagon will surely complain about our absence."

And with those parting words, Push removed his red hat and bowed deeply to the children — as if on stage.

Freedom . Freedom Lost

Like a candle's delicate flame fluttering in a gentle breeze, my essence flickers as freedom slips away like the transition between day and night when light surrenders to darkness — imperceptible — in the briefest of moments.

Daylight, twilight.

He manages, administers, directs, and thinks it his duty, his right — not in meanness, but because he's man.

At times, I feel threatened ... in subtle ways.

Twilight, darkness.

Restraint and fear ensue. Imperceptible change. Indirect. Illusive.

Am I obliged to endure because I'm a woman?

I long for the keyless door. I thirst for my escape. Like a thief in the night, take what I want, out, through the breached portal, into the night.

Darkness.

I don't want to leave. I just want it back. Can he understand? I know he cares. Understand. Try.

He listens and gives me freedom ... to question ... to discover ... to dream.

He listens and gives me freedom ... to think on my own ... to speak ... to choose.

Dawn.

Unbuttoned

Lying on his back, head resting on muscular arms and crisp-white feather-pillow, Anton confidently consumes my nightly preparations. Soft, lucid, cotton nightshirt gathers at my waist. Fragile brown buttons cascade — three unbuttoned to expose pale skin to the cool night-air. His eyes rest there. I mirror his attentive countenance.

He whispers venerable lies about — bright pale-blue eyes that sing a joyful song ... inviting full lips ... abundant hair the color of the midday sun ... long sensual legs ... smooth skin like delicate cloth ... musky scent of meadow flowers moist with spring rain ... a taste of ... always something sweet. Tonight, in the moment, I believe his beautiful lies.

I sit knowingly, expectantly, by his side.

Anton sees wife, mother, friend, and lover. Tender smiles linger. Tonight, I see only him.

My eyes speak ... softly. I need freedom. I need my spirit. My heart beats its nightly, tranquil, rhythmic message ... understand me, please, understand me.

I silence my heart.

I quiet my mind.

I let our eyes meet.

Fingertips touch.

Unbuttoned.

Beautiful lies.

Reflections

My eyes opened with a jolt. I stared at the ceiling. Anton lay with his back to me. I sat up trying to remember why I awakened so abruptly. Gazing blindly at the far wall, it came to me. Trap the wolf. Put him on the train going west. I kept repeating the words.

I nudged my sleeping husband. "Anton, wake up. Wake up, Anton. I must tell you something." He moaned, but he didn't move. I poked his back, lovingly. Again. He knew I wouldn't stop — poke, poke — more groans. "Anton, wake up."

"Emma, please let me sleep," he garbled into his pillow.

I moved over, put my arm around him, and nestled up to his back resting my head on his left shoulder. It would take only a moment.

"Emma, please!"

I moved — slightly. His head turned ... a smile. He rolled onto his back. I rested my head on my right hand and returned his smile.

"Anton, I woke up repeating these words, *trap the wolf* and *take the train going west*. Do you know what that means?"

"You want to go hunting for wolves? You're ... going to sell the pelts ... someplace in the west? I don't know Emma."

"No, Anton. I'm to take charge of ..."

"Oh no, Emma, we both know what happens when you take charge of things. You always get into trouble. You get other people into trouble."

"Yes, but ..."

"I know you will do this, whatever it is, regardless what I say, so tell me exactly what you must take charge of."

"The wedding, America ..."

"What?"

"I must ensure Wolf marries Greta before we leave. I'm destined to organize and direct our efforts to leave Solotoye, to make this voyage to America happen. I can do it Anton. I should do it."

"Of course, Emma, of course." A final resigned *of course* slipped from my, sometimes understanding, husband.

"Are you agreeing because you want to go back to sleep?" He nodded. I kissed him and rolled onto my back staring at the ceiling. I should get an early start to this day. I covered his shoulder with our warm blanket and slipped out of bed into the invigorating chill of a promising spring day. I heard Anton mumble something about two whiskers. I glanced at Peter and Maria sleeping soundly in their berth by the small, shuttered window. They deserve a better life in a new world. I will get this done. I felt motivated ... hopeful.

* * * *

"Father, you talk about going to America. Have you decided if you will go and where you want to settle?" I shoved the fuzzy photograph across the table and smiled.

"What ... who ... who are these women Emma?"

"They're called *Crusaders for Law and Order*, and they're the government in a small village in Kansas called Ellis. You know, where the Rothmans live."

"Sure, the Rothmans, but why ..."

"Because Father, I think this is the place for us. I think you should sell. We should make Ellis our new home."

"I don't know Emma."

"Father, the family should get together to talk about America."

"What does Anton think about this Emma?"

"We haven't talked seriously yet." Father stared at me quizzically. I looked away.

"Sure, Emma, a family meeting ... to talk. I assume you will organize everything — that you will include Push?"

"Of course, Father. I will take care of ... everything." He nodded and smiled.

* * * *

The meeting went well. All expressed enthusiasm about the possibilities of starting a new life in Ellis, but in many ways reluctant to leave our homes, our friends, our way of life on the steppe. After several hours discussing the positive and negative sides of leaving, we kept saying that the move represented hope. It represented the possibility of regaining a little dignity, of reclaiming freedoms taken.

During the discussions, I kept looking at Wolf thinking he surely wanted Greta there with him. I tried dropping subtle hints. 'It will be nice to raise a family in a place that has so much to offer, so much future for the children.' 'We will live together. We will buy and work the land together.' Seeds planted, I told myself. Now, a little moisture, a bit of weeding, a spot of sunshine, and I will harvest a new couple.

Righteous honorable endeavors would produce only good things, I thought, but noble parents, called good intentions, gave birth to an undisciplined child named chaos. It grew quickly and touched the lives of all. What if ... Marta never showed us that photograph? What would have happened then?

In little time, the move to Ellis became Father's passion. One intention accomplished. I nudged and assisted when appropriate. That's all, really. Nudging and assisting with good intentions, but somehow the marriage and move became all twisted and scratchy like cucumber vines. They grew together in a green maze-like world. They became inseparable. Somehow, I lost control of my project. A sticky maze dragged me down. I struggled below green leaves. Scratchy vines wrapped themselves around me until

I could fight no more.

Yet, wonderful news came when Greta told Zees and me that Wolf asked her to marry him. But Greta's acceptance was conditional. She made Wolf promise that if they got married and left Solotoye, he would bring her back. Wolf agreed, telling her that he wanted to make his fortune, return, and buy the tobacco plant. He would build her the biggest stone house in the village. He only needed two, maybe three years. He told her these things. And, because she loved him — she believed him. Greta also told Wolf she should talk to her parents first — before Wolf asked for her father's permission. She knew her father well. Her choice would not make him happy. He wanted someone more mature. He wanted someone older and with money. He didn't want a Zimmer.

The prickly vines twisted, turned, and spread to the Buchs' home. As expected, Greta's father became enraged over the announcement. Her mother watched helplessly. Herr Buchs refused to talk or listen to Greta when she tried to convince him of her love for Wolf. Shortly after Greta told her parents, a chance meeting took place at the tavern between my father, Greta's father, and Push. Herr Buchs overheard Father talking to Push about leaving Solotoye. The idea of the Zimmer family leaving pleased Greta's father. It would remove Wolf from his daughter's life. Smart wealthy men utilize many resources. Herr Buchs decided to help Father with his family's move to America. He attached conditions to his offer to buy Father's property.

The two men met in the empty church exchanging the customary and efficient greeting, *Buchs. Zimmer.* The usual slight nod of the heads accompanied the greetings. Herr Buchs, while thinking how he would begin, watched Father nervously rub the crucifix on his rosary. Greta's father wasted no words. He saved them like rubles.

"Keep your son away from my daughter, and I will buy your property at a price that will allow you to go to America, to pay your debts, make the trip, and get started there. Give me your answer tomorrow."

Greta's father wasted no words. My father spoke no words. He simply licked his lips and thought of celebrating with a drink. His son's interest in Greta got lost in a daydream of rubles, debts marked paid, a wonderful voyage, and new land in a new world. Unfortunately, Father's dream lasted … well, until he saw his son at home.

Wolf, surprisingly, and out of respect for his father, controlled his rage. But he refused to withdraw his proposal, or even to stop seeing Greta. Greta's reaction, when told by Wolf, amounted to a sad, but powerfully explosive mixture of anger and disgust. Multiple explosions ensued. What if? I was still a captive retained in that green maze. I could see and hear everything, but I could do nothing. Things moved quickly.

Commissar Shishkin coiled and struck with a bite that sent Greta's father reeling. The venom spread quickly and dulled Herr Buchs' senses. After a few well chosen words, Shishkin convinced Greta's father that he should betroth his daughter to a man of means and power — to Shishkin himself. In his muddled state, Greta's father agreed.

Herr Buchs announced the betrothal privately to Greta and publicly in church on Sunday. This, however, did not stop the young couple from seeing each other. Greta told her father she would not marry Shishkin. She told him she had rights as a woman in this new century. She told him things were no longer done as they were done in the past — as done by the old people. Greta's father understood one thing. He knew he couldn't force the wedding. He went to the soviet's serpent for help. They shed plan-one like old skin.

The Russian reptile convinced Herr Buchs the only way to rid themselves of Wolf Zimmer was to physically rid themselves of Wolf Zimmer — meaning, they would put his name on a special military service induction list. They did. They added one more name to the short list thinking it more legitimate. The two young men had two weeks to put their affairs in order. They could not appeal.

A new pivotal character entered the story — fate.

In a drunken state, Shishkin accidentally divulged soviet secrets to Push Wiggens. Shishkin bragged of his wealth, his power. Shishkin shocked Push by implying he acquired his, for some, enviable status, by … well, this part was not clear. Shishkin mumbled and slurred words and phrases like — skimmed — cream from milk — a little off the top — payments of some sort — and German helper.

Shishkin, soaked in vodka, arrogance, and ignorance, slithered slowly through tavern's gate seeking a hole into which he could crawl. Push sat and scratched his head wondering what he heard.

Mysterious moments followed. Main and secondary characters played their parts half-dazed. Like Push, they scratched heads in befuddled states. Illogical things happened. Greta's father withdrew the betrothal to Shishkin, and the snake did not protest. Cancelled induction orders came without explanation. And, Greta's father proceeded with his generous offer to buy Father's property, though Wolf and Greta continued their courtship.

Only three could answer the questions never asked. Sometimes, people know, sometimes, a village knows — when to leave things alone. Solotoye stored those secrets like the Volga Hills' forest safeguards the mysteries of countless days and nights.

* * * *

Greta and Wolf formally announced their engagement and their plans to leave Solotoye, which caused Greta's father to disown his daughter. Despite daily attempts to resolve the issue, Greta could not get her father to talk to her. Greta finally joined the Zimmer clan in a modest ceremony. Push Wiggens gave the bride to a handsome and, apparently, happy Wolf Zimmer.

Consequences unintended — amidst preparations for the trip to America, Greta sheepishly and reluctantly announced her pregnancy to the family. Travel schedule, purchased tickets, and selfishness dominated Wolf's behavior. He refused to delay their voyage to America. Greta's delivery would take place onboard a steamship. Greta feared the delivery of her first child.

* * * *

My eyes opened with a jolt. I stared at the ceiling. Anton lay with his back to me. I sat up trying to remember why I awakened abruptly. Gazing blindly at the far wall, a familiar feeling enveloped me. I placed both hands on my flat stomach.

"I'm pregnant," I said softly. A rush of mixed emotions flooded my consciousness ... motherly love ... anxiety ... fear. Will Anton get angry? Will I experience trouble as I did with Maria? The trip ... what about our trip to America? A single tear rolled down my cheek. More followed. I eased myself onto my back and reached for my husband. I touched his arm.

"What's wrong Emma?" He turned to face me. "Emma?"

We held each other's eye contact. We said nothing.

"Emma, are you crying?" I nodded. "What is it?

What's wrong?"

"Anton, I'm pregnant." I could see fear in his eyes, not anger, fear.

"Oh, Emma!"

"Anton, I'm scared. Mother said I could die if I have another baby. It shouldn't have happened. We were ... careful."

He held me and told me everything would be alright. He held me. Silence.

"We should wait," I said barely above a whisper. "We must wait, Anton. The trip ... I can't travel when I'm pregnant."

"Of course. If that's what you want, we'll wait. It will be fine Emma. You're stronger now ... it will be ... fine."

I stared at the ceiling thinking Mayor Wasen and Ellis must wait — only a year. We will wait.

My hands remained on my stomach. Thoughts raced through my head — dying during labor ... losing Anton and the children ... who will take care of them ... fear of death ... not wanting to wait ... will they go without us ... a baby ... a healthy baby ... and how will I tell Zees and Greta?

Zimmers!

Zees, Greta, and I strolled along Little Karman heading for the village. As usual, I started the conversation, "Thinking about leaving Solotoye, strange thoughts pop into my head — things I want to do." I waited for a response. I studied their reactions. "You know what I mean?" They nodded questioningly.

"So, Emma, tell us about those strange thoughts — thoughts that apparently multiply in your head like ... well, you know," said Zees as she shared what I took to be a respectful smirk with Greta.

"Well ... why we never planted shade trees. Look, no shade trees," I pointed to the western horizon, "fruit trees, no cottonwoods, or Chinese elms. Why? We see windmills, the church, and the tops of roofs. I mean ... the summers get unbearably hot. Why didn't we plant shade trees?" I looked at Zees and Greta.

I continued, "And, why do we always close our shutters?" Zees started her response, but I cut her off. "No, I know, to keep out the sun and cold. See, with shade trees, we wouldn't worry about the sun. But even with nice weather, most keep the shutters closed. Why? We know everybody in the village, yet we appear anxious with our neighbors, and we cower at the sight of strangers." They didn't like hearing the truth, so they ignored my blunt statement.

Zees thankfully broke the silence. "Emma, it bothers me that we, most of us, never learned the Russian language. I know, the Kontor keeps us isolated, but we deal with the Russians a lot. We use many of their words, like Matushka, babushka, nushnik, and now ... we think of them as our words. What do you think about that Emma? Greta?"

I waited for Greta to say something, but she just smiled passively. "I agree Zees. And some of the borrowed words we changed, like galushkas. The Russian word sounds similar, but we changed it. We eat their Rossiya chocolate at our weddings, and we drink their Zhiguli beer and Rodnik vodka," I poked Greta in the arm, "when we go to the tavern." We laughed. "The chocolate, beer, vodka, all of it comes from Samara, a city up river never seen because the Kontor doesn't allow us to travel there."

"Greta, what about you? Don't you want to share something?" asked Zees. Greta stared at wispy white clouds without responding. We waited patiently. Annoying silence.

"Church holy days," she blurted out as we waited for an explanation. Nothing.

"What about them?" I asked with a tedious tone, which Greta thankfully missed, or chose to ignore. She finally, grudgingly, continued.

"The men encourage Father Thomas to create special holy days, which become drinking holy days. You know, Saint ... what's his name for the harvest, and ... last year somebody asked Father to establish a special day for Ivan Ivanovich, you know, the thief who, according to our folktales, gave Solotoye its name. How ridiculous!"

"So, Emma, what other entertaining gems muddle that pretty head of yours?" Zees asked in a joking way.

"Well, I would like to eat Kartoffel und Klump in the field one more time. I always look forward to it. After working in the fields, the women getting together to boil the potatoes and cook the dumplings ... the smell of onions cooking in butter ... salt and pepper, such a simple meal. Placing potatoes and dumplings in one big bowl — everybody sits on the ground helping themselves. I will miss eating Kartoffel und Klump in the fields, and I will miss singing after we finish eating." Zees and Greta remained silent as they stared into the fields.

"Oh, Emma, how about this?" exclaimed Zees. "The Kirghiz rugs and the market — I enjoy market when the Kirghiz buy our quilts, sheepskin-coats, and filzstiefel boots. We buy their rugs ... oh, and their camels sometimes. Their ancestors raided our villages when we came to the Volga. That's nice, don't you think? Not the raids, but ..." Greta and I nodded our agreement.

"Good, Zees. We each own one of their rugs. We must take them with us. We, the men, should make the travel trunks larger." We glanced at each other with concern.

I took a deep breath and exhaled — slowly. They gave me questioning looks. "I, ah, want another ... baby." I didn't know how to say … what I wanted to say … what I should say.

"WHAT," shouted Zees. "Emma … you … can't!"

Greta's piercing stare was hurtful. I lowered my head.

"You're pregnant aren't you? You're not going with us," Greta shouted accusingly.

"I should stay …" I studied Greta's face, then Zees' eyes. We stopped walking. "Can we sit by the windmills?" We sat resting weary backs on the backside of the wooden butterflies while looking over the fields. "We will leave when the baby is old enough to travel, when I …" I couldn't say it, but they saw the fear in my face.

"Greta, what are you thinking?" I asked sheepishly. She stared at the golden quack grass, pulled a head from its stem, and twisted the grass between her fingers watching the head twirl. "Greta?"

"You know Emma. I'm pregnant too, but my husband says I must go. That's what I'm thinking Emma. He doesn't consider me or the baby. I'm the one who doesn't want to go, but he … orders me to go. You're the one who wants to go the most, and you get to stay. That's what I'm thinking. Eight months pregnant with my first child when we leave, that's it … that's what I'm thinking. I will birth this baby on a lousy damned ship. It's not sensible. It's not fair. I just want him to … I don't know, but your brother won't listen to his wife. I hope you enjoy your time here Emma. Zimmers!" she grumbled under her breath.

"I heard that Greta."

"Good!"

"Greta, it'll be …" She cut me off.

"Don't! Don't tell me it will be alright. Do not …"

I pleaded with my eyes for Zees to say something, to help me out of this mess. She raised her eyes and shrugged. "Greta, you're right. I don't know, but you're not angry at me. You're angry with yourself for … for marrying Wolf … for getting pregnant … because Wolf is making you go when you're pregnant. I don't blame you for the last two." She looked at me waiting for an explanation. "You married Wolf because you love him."

"Your self-righteous arrogance ... the disgustingly annoying, the amazing Emma Wasen ..." She tried ripping the stem of grass, but couldn't. She wildly threw it to the side. Chaffing, she kicked at it. Her head dropped and her breathing shortened. Her face flushed.

"He's your husband Greta," I said in a whisper. "None of them behave as we would like. Our behavior certainly puzzles them at times — most of the time. If older, maybe he would see it differently. I don't know." I looked to Zees again.

"You won't do this alone Greta. The ship employs a doctor. Remember the papers they gave us?" Zees' comments relieved me. They made a difference. Greta gazed at her as if to ask her to say more things like that. "Anna and I will help you," Zees added. Greta considered Zees' comforting thoughts for a moment.

"I'm sorry," Greta responded softly. "I'm feeling sorry for myself again. I love him, and I must take the good with the bad. We say it in our vows. I can ... I will do this." Greta glanced at the two of us with conviction and held out her left hand. We took it gladly and pulled her to us. We hugged awkwardly. We laughed at our contorted bodies. I let go and rolled into the grass.

"Zimmers!" exclaimed Greta jokingly while forcing a laugh.

Once Upon A Shade Tree

As children,
We wish for many things.
When I was taller than three,
I wished for a shade tree.

Father dug a sapling from river's bank.
He helped prepare it's new home —
Made space in soil colored red
For fragile, moist roots to spread.

I tucked them in gently, lovingly.
I tamped reddish clay soil,
Layer after layer,
As Father whispered a prayer.

I gave it plenty to drink,
But Father said,
Not too much, I think.

On the southwest corner
She did stand —
Leaves wilting,
Needing a hand.

I watched her.
I nursed her.
I gave her my all.

I went to her,
Even without a call.

But Father said,
It wasn't meant to be.
It's God's will
You see.

An honorable attempt
We made.
But my house remains
Without shade.

Touch Everything

I notice Stay's eyes as I watch Push and Stay from the window. Fear, confusion, and sadness moisten the dry, cold, December air. Push picks up his old friend and holds him as he always does — front paws over left shoulder — always the left shoulder. Push presses his head to Stay's ... gently. Stay responds by licking Push's ear. Stay always licks Push's ear.

* * * *

How can I do this? Will I find the strength to hand him to Emma? Push asks himself. He knows only this place — Wiggens' Place. Emma already holds his blanket — little more than a rag now. She told me she would put it on their wagon seat, like here. She will. He will ... love Emma too. Is it crazy to love an animal so much?

Heinrich and Jacob will take good care of Pull. Emma waits. One more walk around the yard. I need to touch everything ... touch one more time. Stay usually doesn't let me carry him this long. He wants to go with me.

Wagon teasingly complains about me leaving, but I know she will miss me. Touch. Fingers don't want to let go. Shed door — I rub the rusty latch. I feel the broken board — broken since ... well, too long to remember. I smell Pull's leather harness. Apple trees — I planted when? Garden waiting for spring. Small barn needs paint. I was going to do that next year. I run my hand along the birch fence. How many times did I repair it? How many trips to Matushka for wood? I look back to the house, my ancestor's house, and feel guilt. Will Buchs honor his promise? Will he keep the thatched roof? Will he find somebody to run the tavern? I give a last glance to — the church across River Road — the table where Greta and Emma sat that Sunday afternoon — the uneven bench I wanted to fix, but the men joked about it so much I decided to leave it. Touch it. It still wobbles. I force myself up three crooked steps, too cold to creak, to the door. I lovingly press my hand to it. I turn the keyless latch. It opens.

My eyes slowly scan the bedroom where Helga gave birth to Zelma, where Helga died. Emma waits in the kitchen. I go there. Stay's claws still cling to my coat. I tell myself to ... be strong. I tell myself not to cry, but ... Throat and heart ache. I tell myself not to cry ...

* * * *

I force myself up from the table. Weepy eyes, that cannot bear to look, meet. I gently pull Stay's claws from Push's coat and willingly take Stay because I know Push cannot. Stay's eyes question Push ... but Stay knows. I pull the door closed behind us. The hardest thing.

Saying Goodbye

We stood awkwardly in the crowded schoolhouse amidst friends and family not knowing what to say. Thin air pressed heavy hearts. Greta kept checking the door hoping to see her father. She didn't want to leave without ... she didn't want to leave.

I tugged at Greta's arm. "A small gift for you." I handed her a package — writing paper folded into a small square, tied with plain string, a bow on top. "Don't open it until you get to Ellis." She hugged me. "When you get there, send us a picture of the three of you." I patted her stomach.

"I'll send a photograph. You'll leave after the baby is born, right? You and the baby will be fine Emma. We pray for you."

"I know. As soon as the baby can travel." I noticed Greta watching the door again. "He still loves you Greta. He'll get over it. Who knows, maybe your family will come with us. I'll keep talking to your mother — to Heinrich and Jacob."

"Father will never leave Solotoye, Emma." Greta placed the package carefully in her pocket and hugged me again.

"It's time to go," Father announced to the gathering. His voice broke. He cleared his throat and repeated the words. The words caught in his throat.

Greta gave her mother a last hug, kissed her on the cheek, and stared into her weeping eyes. "Just two years — we'll see each other in two years. Tell Father I love him." Greta reluctantly pulled herself from her mother's arms. She hugged Heinrich and Jacob. Greta walked unwillingly to the open door holding desperately onto her mother and brothers. The laden wagons waited.

I watched Mother and Father climb onto their wagon. I don't know why, but I counted. Nine are leaving, I said to myself. My throat ached. My tears fell uncontrollably. I held Mother's hand. "We'll see you soon — a year," I said softly. Wheels turned. They groaned under their burden. I moved with them — trying to smile, trying to stay with them. "I love you." The simple gaunt words were inaudible. My hand slipped from hers. Father reached for me, hands trying, but not touching. I held onto the wagon as I walked. Eyes remained locked and images burned my mind. A familiar gentle grasp whispered its reluctant message. I stopped.

Separation — my mind measured the distance, the growing gap between us. Faint images blurred like stirring fluid shadows. I watched until they disappeared. Weak shadows vanished.

I silently called out their names — Mother ... Father ... Bernard, Zees, Helga, Walter ... Push, Wolf ... Greta.

Father ... Mother.

Mother?

The sounds of family flood my consciousness as Stay
and I walk the short distance to my parents' house.

Laughter, singing, cooking,
Yelling,
Banging of pots and pans,

And the
Welcomed sound of silence,

Sneezing, coughing, praying,
Crying,
Crackle of burning wood,

And the
Welcomed sound of silence,

Eating, cleaning, chatter,
Snoring,
Footsteps on creaking floorboards,

Children fighting, deep sighs,
And the
Welcomed sound of silence.

I step into the cold entry with Stay clinging to my side. I say "Hello," as I always did. From distant corners, the word accosts me. Scares me. "Hello, hello." My heartbeat quickens. Dazed, I lean forward and peer through the open door.

"Mother?" I ask softly, quizzically.

Silence answers … yet, I listen. I wait to hear her voice.

Silence.

Cautiously, I glance into the kitchen and my parents' bedroom. Why am I afraid? I came to be close to them. Breathing deeply, I push the bedroom door to see what … who is there. My feet don't move. Reality — gone — but not. Respectfully, I step into their room. I probe crisp winter air with gloved hand trying to touch them. Pausing by the foot of their bed, I clutch ethereal air. I gently press it to my chest hoping to sense them.

I settle on the edge of the bed smoothing the comforter. Stay joins me sniffing unfamiliar scents. He crawls onto my lap. Stay looks into my eyes with concern, and he settles his warm body onto my lap to comfort me. I lay my hand on his back, and I begin to relax — to accept my family's presence.

I scan the room haltingly. A smile lightens my face as I notice Mother's cleaning — floors, windows, everything. Family photographs are no longer on the wall, but the Tsar's photograph and cross remain. Choices, I say to myself.

Photographs — Greta promised to send one with her first letter. How long will it be? They said they would write. They would tell us everything. They would tell us about — the land and people in Ellis, what to expect on our voyage — everything. It's only been one day, but I'm already anticipating their letters. I long to hear from them. It will be months before ... two, maybe three months.

Stay jumps the three steps and races to the gate as I close the door.

"I'll see you ... soon." Smiling, I press my hand to the door.

Stay waits at the gate begging me to chase him. Playfully, I lunge. He readies to pounce ... then bursts into the street.

Memories and Impressions

March, 1902

Dearest Emma, Anton, and Children,

We send our love and hope this letter finds all of you in good health. A little girl named Anna joyfully joined the Zimmer family. As you can see in the photographs, Greta, Wolf, and daughter Anna radiate happiness and good health. We hope and pray that you, Emma, find strength and that your pregnancy comes to term with no problems for you or the baby.

We have much to tell you. First, we miss you and our beautiful Solotoye. We remember the trip as long, difficult, but also exciting. Many new and wonderful things warmed our bodies and souls. They filled us like a full granary. The voyage affected each of us differently. Each remembers different things. We now tell you a few special memories and impressions of the trip and America.

Temperatures on the trains and ships skated between chilly and icy. Passengers created interesting ways to stay warm. You should travel in warmer weather when you come to America. The trains in Russia rock from side-to-side like boats on Matushka in stormy weather. The unnecessary hurry of trains makes it difficult to see what passes by the window. Blink and you miss a meadow, a lake, or man in his field with rake.

Our train stopped in Warsaw. At an Inn close to the

train station, we ate dinner. Anna, Zees, and Greta say they could get used to no cooking and no cleaning of dishes. The men talk about the cost.

We crossed the Atlantic Ocean on the SS Frankfurt. The ship's doctor told us the SS stands for Steam Ship. We don't know if he joked or not. Our metal ... boat, bigger than any ships on Matushka Volga, thankfully remained ... afloat. The ocean crossing stayed storm-free. We thanked God.

The city of New York and its harbor amazed us. A new statue, taller than three or four windmills, sits in the harbor. The unknown, beautiful lady holds a torch. We don't know why they put a statue in the middle of the harbor. A new building that is, by our guess, twice as tall as the steeple of Solotoye's beautiful church rises above other tall buildings in the city, like a ... steeple. Ellis Island also sits in the harbor. There, officials checked papers, doctors gave physical examinations, and Greta gave birth to Anna. The island and our new home share the same name. This amused us.

As our ship continued south from New York, we passed a city called Miami that has miles of beautiful sandy beaches and summer temperatures in January. Our ship turned and followed the sun as we sailed into the Gulf of Mexico towards our final stop of Galveston, which also has warm weather in winter. One could get used to this kind of weather.

The strange language, English, makes processing at the ports difficult. You must listen carefully for your name and go where the, sometimes rude, men point. Many of the names they do not say correctly. We thought it a miracle that we got on the right trains.

Newsboys on trains in America sell many interesting things — newspapers written in English, books of all kinds — some would require a trip to the confessional if purchased — fruit, and candy called lollipops. Bernard bought two for the children. Wolf bought cigars for the men. The newsboys also sell soap, towels, dishes, pitchers made of tin, coffee, tea, sugar, and food called hash.

Unlike Solotoye, few people and buildings reside in Ellis, although a friendly calmness exists in this tiny village. A small stream trickles through the town. Greta and Zees call it Klein Matushka. Little Mother gives life to the trees and animals. People of Ellis call this stream Big Creek. We find this funny.

People from Russia live north of Klein Matushka in a place called Rooshin Town. They make fun of people from Russia, but we ignore them. Many families live in houses on their land a long distance from the village — a peculiar custom.

A large red-brick building, where trains are repaired, sits to the south of the Rothman's house — across Klein Matushka. Tracks for the trains run through the middle of the village. Bernard and Wolf will try to get work for the railroad — *a road made with rails we call it.*

Land around Ellis looks like the land in Solotoye — flat, dry, and no trees. And like Solotoye, the winters become cold. Herr Rothman told us the summers get hot and the wind blows too much and too hard. Land costs more than we thought. Free land in Ellis County no longer remains. Much of the land sits idle, not producing crops, so opportunity knocks on our door like a welcomed visitor.

We will write again soon. When you write, please send your letters to the Rothman's address, which you have. Please write soon. We are anxious to hear about your health Emma. We pray that you are still with us.

The Zimmer Family and Push Wiggens

Things Not Said

May 1902

To My Dear Mother and Father,
My Sweet Brothers and Sisters-in-Law, and
Our Dear Friend Push Wiggens,

Thank you so much for your letter and photographs. We rejoice that you made it to America in good health, and we welcomed the news about the birth of the newest Zimmer. Anna obviously inherited beauty from her mother and her father.

Anton and I remain confident concerning my delivery. Do not worry, I take care of myself and the baby, who kicks constantly and lovingly. Mother Wasen kindly does my chores — no laundry for Emma.

We loved the information about Ellis, but what about Mayor Mary Wade? You promised to write about her. Have you met her and the other women? Please tell me about her in your next letter.

Greta, I know your mother, father, and brothers wrote to you. They surely told you about trying to reach you at the Saratov train station before you left. Your father forgave you Greta. They reached the platform of the station only to see the end of your train in the distance. They called to you, but the train made much noise and already traveled a fair distance. He loves you Greta.

Solotoye lacks interesting, or even any, news. Every-thing goes as it did before you left. The young Miller family moved into our house — the Zimmer house. The house begged for a new family. Houses should not be empty.

Anton and I do small things every week preparing for our voyage to America. As you suggested, we will try to make the trip in spring or summer.

Please write soon. Wishing you all the best from,

Emma, Anton, Peter, and Maria Wasen

Inside . Under . Beyond

How many times have I done this — peel potatoes, slice potatoes, boil potatoes, stir dough until arm hurts, little dollops scooped and placed in with the potatoes, watch dumplings form in boiling pot, prepare frying pan with butter and onion? How many times? I cook without thinking, at least without thinking about cooking. What I do think about when standing in the kitchen peeling, slicing ... puzzles me.

I get inside my head to see what lingers there. I get under my skin to sense my feelings. I go beyond the Emma everybody sees. I peel back the skin, stir up the contents, and watch what happens.

Why can't I look out the window when peeling and slicing? Why must the blue shutters remain closed? The sun doesn't come in this window. Why blue? It's such a pale blue. I like red. Red energizes. When will Anton fix the wooden handle on this knife?

Anton. Oh, my Anton. My handsome husband understands me, but he doesn't understand me. He loves me. I know he loves me, but ...

Like snowflakes, all dumplings differ in size and shape. I watch steam rise and disappear. The trick — make the dumplings soft — not hard and chewy. I don't know how much time they take. I simply know when to take them off the fire, even when thinking such crazy things.

Anton loves me, but he considers me too strong for a woman and too independent for his liking. I love his energy. He always busies himself doing something, except fixing the handle on this knife. He finds time for us — gentle words whispered in my ear, a caress while working in the garden or fields. Losing me remains his biggest fear. I am stronger. I almost died with Maria. *Stronger now*, I repeat the words — until I believe them.

Interesting thing about cooking kartoffel und klump in big black pan — no need to call the family. Sizzle and smell bring them to the table. They sit. They wait. Peter and Maria with fork in hand — sitting and waiting. Standing behind me, Anton grabs what used to be my waist. He lovingly runs his hand over my stomach and lingers for a moment.

"You shouldn't be cooking Emma. Let Mother do the work." I smile, kiss his cheek gently, and give him the first dumpling with my ladle. The dumpling looks like the sandbar at the river — the one we see from our ...

Another meal eaten in silence. Do all families do this? Why can't we talk during the meal? I hear the endless scraping of tin forks on tin plates, chewing of food, milk being swallowed, glasses slammed back to the table, Father Wasen belching, Peter's muffled laugh, then his imitation. Maria tries to hold in a giggle. I try to hide my smile as I look for Anton's reaction, usually his reprimand of PETER, which he doesn't mean. Why do I hear these things?

Every meal I hear scraping tin on tin, chewing, swallowing, slamming, and belching.

Anton and Father Wasen will leave for the tavern shortly. I must rest. Repeat the words, *I am stronger.*

"I am ..."

Things not said.

Limestone Gateway

Though unseen, I have a clear vision of this place called Ellis County. I paint a picture dense with detail absorbed from the few letters received from my family — detail of my devise. Of all the beautiful and unusual things, I focus on the walled gateway made from native limestone. Bernard described the stone as pale-yellow with imprints of dead sea animals and markings from holes used to split the rock — into blocks for buildings and posts for fences.

When I'm there, Bernard will show me the imprints of the sea animals. I will ask him about stone cutting and about masons. Wolf said the entrance to their property starts at the county road. The portal, or pathway, putters a short distance south before it curves gently to the right, then it slides south following a line of old cottonwoods. It sounds beautiful when I write it. I can see the yellow stone wall rising three or four feet from new green grass. The wall parallels the gateway. Bernard and Wolf cut the tall grass on both sides of the wall with scythes. I smell the cut grass. Father watches proudly as his sons build their new home in America.

An intermittent stream trickles into the property from the south and exits northeast of the newly built house. When the stream runs full, it eventually finds its way to the Saline River just a mile north. Naturally, the cottonwoods border the brook's careless course. The limestone house sits on a small hill above and to the west of the stream. The peaceful setting borrows cottonwood shade in summer and protection from winter's menacing months from nearby hills.

Coyotes sing to the yellow ball in the blue-black, starlit summer sky. I hear the hound's prairie song. I see her silhouetted against the setting lunar orb. Her head tilts back and mouth opens. She sits on hind legs — comfortable and at home. Three pups yelp trying to mimic their mother.

North of Stonewall Ranch, a harvest moon throws its yellow light on resting woods along the Saline's shallow waters. Sandbars soak up the beams while its rock crystals reflect the borrowed light — such a pretty and restful sight.

Shade your eyes as you gaze into the sun-drenched field. A team of huge healthy horses pulls the peasant's plow through sod exposing soil black as coal. Arms and hands made of steel guide the simple tool. Black earth and shards of grass stick to the man's sunburned sweating skin. The field stretches wide and long. He stops to rest and canvasses his field — turned prairie grass and what remains. He wipes his brow with his sleeve smiling proudly.

High, filmy, scattered clouds in an azure afternoon sky provide a beautiful background for prairie hawks soaring above the man and his team. His work precludes him from watching. Hawks glide on warm currents with ease. Their vision and power inspire. They dive, climb, spread their wings, and screech. They do many wonderful things. I envy them. Telescopic eyes follow the man with arms of steel hoping he scares up a meal.

Rabbits abound, some with tails made of cotton, others called Jack. Greta said, "In Ellis County, both are found." Prairie hawk watches with interest. Dogs chase them, but soon lose interest. They sit. They hide. They dash about famously to save their hide. Many will lose their pelt. They multiply quickly, so the loss is little felt.

In this wonderland, the Zimmer family makes their home. They call this dwelling Stonewall Ranch because my younger brother likes the sound of the words. Stonewall Ranch rests amongst cottonwoods and a rivulet of sparkling clear water.

I will go there. My time approaches. Amble proudly through the Zimmer gateway, touch the limestone wall, smell the freshly cut grass, and embrace my family.

Can't Stop Smiling

"Do you have a buyer for the shop tools ... what about the land?" I asked Anton trying to calm my excitement by talking.

"If Josef borrows from his father, he will buy the tools, workbenches, materials ... everything. Tomorrow, Herr Koenig will give me his answer about the land. And, if Koenig doesn't buy the land, Father said he would. We don't have to worry Emma."

"I can't believe it, Anton, America. I know Mother and Father Wasen don't understand, but I can't stop smiling ... I can't stop talking. I feel bad that they will no longer see the children. They enjoy them so much."

"Yes, the children will miss them, I will ..." He cleared his throat and continued. "I thought I could convince Father to go with us, but ... he believes you must be young to go to America — to start over. I think he understands why we must go. Mother doesn't understand, but she will. Did you put the travel papers in the trunk?"

"I did. Anton, are you happy ... you know, that we're finally going to America?"

"Yes, Emma. We can build a good business ... in Ellis. Bernard and Wolf said new houses and buildings go up everyday. I know I don't smile as much as you, but I am happy. We must think about the children's future."

I watch Anton as he pretends to work on a customer's

order. I can tell that his mind roams. He moves boards from one place to the other for no apparent reason. I watch his young strong hands. I hope he doesn't go to America just for me. The photograph of Mayor Mary caused me to plead, urge, and petition him. I begged. I want to live in a place that elects women to govern their village. No more Kontor to tell us what to do every minute of every day.

We will join my family and Push in Ellis. We will see Anna. They will see Little Anton.

I spend time with Greta's brothers, Heinrich and Jacob, and with her mother and father. Her father has changed ... and now we all go to America together. Herr Buchs accepted my father's offer to stay at their home until they get settled. How things change ... why things change.

"Anton, do you think Little Anton will be alright?"

"Yes, Emma, for the hundredth time, yes. I'm sure he will be fine. Greta told us what to do, what not to do, and what to take on the trains and ship. He'll be fine."

"How long will you work?" He still moves boards around. He gives me a look that tells me to leave. He needs solitude. Should I tell him he already moved that board three times? Smiling again. He knows me well.

"Go ahead, Emma, say it."

I return his smile, wink, and leave. I love him, and I can't stop smiling. As I walk away, I stop, turn around, and head back to my husband — skirt swinging. I kiss him. Can't stop ...

Send A Telegram

I know how my family felt leaving Solotoye. No, on second thought, it's not the same. They wait for us there. It's not the same. But the feelings of leaving, they must be the same. Greta left her whole family. Her family sits crowded in the wagon ahead of us on their way to live with their daughter, son-in-law, and with their first grandchild, Anna. Greta's mother showed me the photograph of Wolf, Greta, and Anna as if I saw it for the first time.

"See my granddaughter. I'm going to see my grand-daughter," she kept repeating.

I turned and looked one more time at rooftops, steeple, and windmills. Tavern's gate — I can't see it. I don't know why I always think of it. I feel the smoothness of the wood and the coolness of the metal latch. Rooftops, steeple, and windmills get smaller. They become a blur. I blinked to clear my eyes — gone.

I hope my milk lasts. This long trip requires ... don't worry, I tell myself. The road ahead, not much of a road, more like a trail with wagon wheel tracks, pulls us away. The lack of late spring snows provides a passable, but rutty River Road. Our first time on a train, first time on a ship, I say to myself. I remember the letter about the stop in ... Warsaw — where they ate a meal by the train station. I hope we can do that. It sounds nice.

I wonder ... what will I write about the trip. I'll make

notes as we go. Anton bought extra paper, pens, and ink for me. I looked at my husband. He returned my glance with a questioning smile. I playfully bumped his shoulder with mine, put my arm around him, and rested my head on his shoulder. I squeezed him tight. Comfort. Protection. Love.

* * * *

The ferry across the river scared me, but I fixed my eyes ahead, on the city of Saratov. I didn't look down, but I could hear the raging water. *The ferry was scary.* I'll tell Father. Make note of it. The big city sits on the right bank of a very wide and muddy Matushka Volga.

We put our baggage on the train and found seats next to each other. Dusty streams of light flooded the compartment. They landed on the opposite wall and floor. How did Greta manage during the winter? As we pulled away from the station, the train started to rock as if it was going to fall over. We stared at each other. I reached for Peter and Maria while holding onto Little Anton. Greta's father stuck his head out the window and glanced back towards the station. He eased himself back onto his seat and caught Greta's mother's knowing look. After a short distance, we settled into a rhythm that was ... not comforting, but familiar.

* * * *

Our train rolled and rocked its way across Russia. At first, the pace of the train pleased me because it didn't slow for curves. But, as time elapsed and miles mounted, I wanted more speed. When we approached curves, the sight of endless tracks ahead fascinated me. The metal pathway intrigued me. What lies around the bend? I wanted to see everything, but my brain could not process it all. I wanted to go … to where the metal tracks were taking me. I felt alive. A burning sensation settled in the pit of my stomach — Ellis and Mayor Mary Wade. I made it happen. What are Mother and Father doing right now at … Stonewall Ranch? I will see the Saline River they talked about in their letters, and Big Creek in Ellis, and …

* * * *

"Anton, wake up."

"What now Emma? What is it this time? I'm trying to sleep."

"I know you're trying to sleep. I'm sorry, but didn't Wolf and Greta tell us to send a telegram? I can't believe I forgot. I don't even know what that is. Anton, do you know what a telegram is? And, where do we send it? Is it too late?"

"No, Emma, it's not too late. We send the telegram when we get to Galveston port in America. We let them know when we expect to leave Galveston and when we should arrive in Ellis. The train station in Galveston will give us that information. We send it there — at the train station in Galveston. Do you know how long it will be before we get to Galveston?"

"No, but I'm guessing it's not tonight."

"Emma, we are somewhere in Poland, but I'll let you know when we get close to Galveston. I would like to get some sleep. When you finish feeding Little Anton, you should sleep too."

* * * *

"Anton, the man said Warsaw is our next stop. Do you have our papers ready?"

"I don't think we need papers at this stop — only when we enter a country."

"Oh. Can we eat something at this stop? We should buy something. It's not time to eat, but ..."

"Yes, we need a break. We should get out and stretch our legs. Besides, we may change trains here because the next country is Germany. And on the other side of Germany is the port of Bremen where we take the ship across the ocean."

"What are the soldiers doing Anton?" He didn't answer. "They're telling us to follow. They probably want to check our papers. See, they want our travel papers."

"We're from Solotoye, the lower Volga," Anton told the officer.

"Why don't you speak Russian? You're foreigner."

"I speak Russian," replied Greta's father as he stepped

forward to help. "Is there a problem?"

"Your papers are not valid. You cannot travel on these papers. You will return to your homes."

"Buchs, what's going on?" asked Anton.

Soldiers pushed us towards the baggage car. When Greta's father told us what the officer said, we looked at each other, but said nothing. The soldiers didn't care that I was carrying a baby. They pushed me along with the others. Peter and Maria held onto my skirt asking why the angry men shouted. I couldn't answer them.

We huddled in the station with trunks gathered around us, not knowing what to do, not knowing if there was anything we could do. We exchanged bewildered scared glances with other families ... families like us traveling from Saratov. They looked to us for answers. I felt humiliated — as if I was less of a person than the Russian soldiers. Would they really shoot me if I got back on the train, I asked myself? I looked to Anton. His fists clenched. He wanted to solve the problem, but knew he couldn't. I put my arm around him ... told him it would be alright. I glanced down to his hands again. I took his hand in mine.

"Anton ... Anton, look at me, please look at me. You can't solve this. Nobody can change this," I whispered to my proud husband as a tear rolled down his cheek. "We can try again later. Surely this is a mistake. We'll try again later." He reluctantly nodded.

We stood quietly, angrily, waiting for someone to tell us

what to do. Men with rifles and hate etched on their faces guarded the door. Why? Why did they hate us? We are Russians. We produce grain. Did they know we produce grain for them to eat? Men prepared the train to leave. Waving hands signaled the engine. I heard the familiar churning, causing cars to jerk, one after the other. Wheels turned. I handed the baby to Anton.

"Emma, don't!" Anton whispered as he tried to hold me back. "Emma, please!"

I walked towards the door staring at the guard. He moved as if to stop me, but I continued walking daring him to block my way. He watched as I passed through the door. I needed to see our train. Large wheels turned. No, it was more than seeing the train. Dignity forced me there. I moved to the edge of the platform and watched our train pull away. It disappeared. Empty tracks to the west — I followed them with my eyes until two gray steel lines merged into one and bent to the left. I turned and stared at the steel lines going east. They looked the same, but not the same. I looked back through the door. My eyes found Anton and the huddled group. They had not moved. I thought of the stories of our ancestors when they came to Russia. I thought how men with guns escorted them to Solotoye.

Will it be the same? I asked myself.

Foreigner's Papers

June 1904

Dear Family and Friends in America,

You most likely have been concerned about us since you did not receive our telegram. We remain in good health, but the most terrible news we must write. They stopped our train in Warsaw, and after checking our travel papers told us to remove our baggage. The angry soldiers treated other families from the lower Volga the same. After much confusion, they told us we could not travel with our papers. They told us to return to our homes. We tried to explain that we sold our property, and that we could not go back. They didn't listen. That night, they put us on a train going east to Saratov.

We managed to get our property back. So we still have our land, homes, and other things. We asked to travel at a later time, but received a troubling answer. Travel papers of foreigners have been suspended. We are now considered foreigners. We hope the Tsar will change this policy, so we can leave Russia. We pray this letter finds you all in good health.

The Buchs Family
Anton and Emma Wasen

Massive Metal Nails . Gray Rusting Rails

July 1904

Dear Family in America,

I spent many hours trying to process what happened to us. I can't begin to tell you the feelings we all experienced in Warsaw and on the trip back to Solotoye. They consisted of a bewildering mixture of sadness, despair, confusion, hate and ... hope. On the long trip home, I used the seemingly endless hours to explore those feelings, and to jot down thoughts so I could write. When I make an attempt, a vision intrudes — gray steel lines stretching into the distance until two become one — lines going west — lines going east — lines going there — lines coming back. The unsolicited, unwanted mental photograph of those gray steel lines challenges my thoughts.

They squeezed us together in that building, wound tight, wound together with our baggage like string on a ball — shame, insignificant, and foreign. Afraid to speak, afraid to move, fear held us motionless and speechless. Our train slipped between distant buildings and disappeared. I stood at platform's edge staring down at tracks. At that moment, I thought to myself, I'm not Russian. I don't speak the language. They called me a foreigner because I am. One hundred thirty years as foreigners — sad.

Fear kept me from turning around. It's a bad dream,

I told myself. When I open my eyes, will I be on our train going west? Will I see myself in the station having dinner with family and friends? The lines to the west and east symbolized my linear, frail existence — gliding forward, painful steps back — west, east. West was our future. Our past was in the east.

In the briefest of moments it changed. West may still be our future, but east is our past, our present, and possibly our future. Greta, Zees, Bernard, Wolf, I can't let it be our future.

Please help me find the positive. Please help us define our future. I see inviting soft lines reaching towards a warm setting sun. We must make it happen.

Emma

Gifts On Christmas Morning

March 1905

To Our Dearest Family and Friends in America,

We trust that everyone in America remains in good health, especially Mother and Father. I miss you more than I can say. Hopefully, we will see each other soon. I do believe.

I apologize for my last letter. My personal problems should not be written for all to know and suffer. I'm sorry. Thank you Greta and Zees for the special letter titled, Ivan's Gold on Open Prairie. I especially appreciate the effort you put into the title. The beautiful words provoke thought. Thank you. The descriptions of Stonewall Ranch and Ellis inspire me. I read it over and over to Anton and the children. Greta, your family also enjoyed the letter, but I suspect they told you already.

We continue to ask about our travel papers, but the painful answer persists like a bad cold in winter. We shall try again and again.

In the meantime, we must live our lives, and hopefully make the best of our reality in Solotoye. Of course, you do the same in America. I made changes in my life to help me enjoy Solotoye again.

After our experience in Warsaw, it took time to adjust. On the morning of Christmas Day, I went for a walk end-

ing in Father's fields. Snow covered the steppe. I embraced my thoughts and nature. Beauty surrounded me. I started to think clearly. Interesting how nature gives us clarity. I discovered many things about myself that morning.

I realized I need a purpose — a purpose that gives my life meaning beyond wife and mother. I talked to Mother Wasen about this, and she surprisingly agreed to do some of my chores so I can pursue my new goals.

I must analyze my emotions, pose questions, write more, write better. Things inside me need to get out. Like Father, I have many things to say. I want to express them in writing. I'm not suggesting I have answers to life's questions. Sometimes, it's enough to pose the questions.

Two other gifts came to me Christmas morning. First, I realized the children no longer have a storyteller. Push, I will try to carry on your tradition and your folktales. Herr Hohgan said I could tell our stories to the children during school.

The second gift relates to the pleasure I get playing marbles with the children. I decided that I should continue playing with the boys, and I should encourage the girls to learn the games. Maybe, I will combine marbles with storytelling. Anton agreed to provide a few marbles and a leather sack for any child that wants them. Mother Wasen said she would make the sacks. I'm busy with my plan. Hopefully, I'm productive.

Please write soon. Tell us about the children and if

more Zimmer's are on the way. Anton and I would like more children, but ... we must be happy with Peter, Maria, and Little Anton.

Again, I hope this letter finds all in good health. We hope to see you soon.

Emma and Anton

Ten Hands Up For Rats

At first, the girls said yes to learning how to play marbles because they liked the small, soft, tanned-leather pouch with leather drawstring. And they treasured the pretty clay marbles that appeared to be baked in saturated shades of summer and spring, tinted in winter's white, and blazed with fall tones. They often smelled the leather and let the marbles roll around in their small hands. The little clay balls were smooth to the touch.

As they mastered the games, the smelling and handling started to wane for some of the girls. For others, keeping skirts clean and all marbles in the bag became the objective. A few girls learned that *friendlies* ensured them of keeping all their marbles. They agreed to play only if they could play *friendlies* because at the end of *friendlies* — all marbles lost were returned. They studied other girls as they won and lost prized marbles. They were convinced that their way equalled smart — no risk. However, they also noticed the excitement of the other players. Watching these young girls, I learned valuable things about winning and losing, about risk, about being conservative, about the relative importance of clean skirts. We learned together.

"Girls, who can tell me what we call this line, and what we do at the line?" Nine hands shot into the air at the same time. Everybody knew the answer to the easy question. "Amelia."

"It's the pitch line, Frau Wasen."

"Right. And what do we …"

"Oh, sorry. We lag a marble to the other line — the lag line. The one who gets closest to the line goes first."

"Very good, Amelia, and please call me Emma. It's a rule in marbles. You must call your teacher by her first name." The girls laughed. "Fine. It's not a real rule. It's an Emma Rule, and you would please Emma if you obeyed her rule."

"Yes, Frau Wasen," the girls shouted teasingly.

"Well! Just for that, I think we need another Emma Rule." Heads shook jokingly. "Emma Rule number two — before beginning a game, players must pick up a large handful of dirt and throw it on the front of their skirt. Don't worry, it will come out in the wash."

"Bertha, do you have a question? By the way Bertha, no need to raise your hand to ask a question. This isn't school."

"Frau … ah, Emma, doesn't the teacher have to follow the rule also?"

"Yes, yes, yes," the girls shouted. "Teachers too."

"Fine." I grabbed a pinch of dirt, sprinkled it on the hem of my skirt, and started to lag. Shaking heads registered their disapproval. "Fine." I scooped and scraped until my right hand over-flowed with powdery dirt. I threw it as hard as I could. My skirt instantly turned a dusty-brown. A large dirt-cloud covered my shoulders and head.

I choked and frantically waved my hands about trying to clear the air. My shooter sailed from my hand like an oversized clay-shell striking Amelia's head. The errant shooter dropped silently to our dusty marble deck, the inaudible thud muffled by the girls' uncontrollable laughter.

"RATS," moaned Amelia.

"What?" I asked still choking.

"Use rats," said Amelia picking up my shooter while rubbing the side of her head. "My mother said we should say rats in situations like this."

"Rats it is Amelia. Thank you for the suggestion. Let's make it a rule. When something bad happens in marbles, we say RATS. We'll make this Amelia Rule number one. Everybody in favor, raise your hand." Ten hands up for rats.

"Emma?"

"Yes, Rosa."

"Why do all girls' names end with the letter 'a'? Boys' names have different endings. It puzzles me."

"That's a good question — always good to ask questions. It's a custom. I don't know how or why it started, but all girls names do end with an 'a'. Interesting!"

"Emma?"

"Yes, Helena."

"I have a question too."

"Is it about marbles Helena?"

"Yes. Well, I was wondering, if this isn't school, why

you call yourself teacher?" The tall, skinny girl stood erect with a devilish smile, hands in her skirt pockets, rocking heel to toe. I smiled while thinking to myself, oh my, it's me in a smaller package.

"Another good question. The answer is … you're right. If this isn't school, and it isn't, then I'm not your teacher. So, that would make me a … what? Let's call me … ah … I've got it! I'm Emma the Marble Master!

Who wants to play rings, potsies, or five hole? Does everybody remember the rules?"

"YEEEEEES."

"Katherina, your skirt looks too clean to play marbles. Remember Emma Rule number two?" I watched as she grabbed the smallest amount of dirt she could and gingerly spread it down the front of her gray skirt. "Good. Now, you look like a marble player. You know girls, after a few more weeks of practice, you should play with the boys."

"YUK. No, Emma, not boys!"

Folktales

I read to Solotoye's children. I tell them stories in the schoolhouse and under a tree. I go to them because they need me.

Many tales told — *Man in a Red Hat, Horse, Wagon and Cat* — *River Bandit's Gold* — *Barn's Black Door* — *Matushka's Galushkas* — and more. I read to them from Brothers Grimm — morals and messages from tale's trim. We learn about evil and ... good, wrong and right, from a tale of a girl in a ... hood. We laugh, yearn, wonder, and question. We learn.

Kinder und Hausmärchen — tattered cover, pages soiled and frayed, tales fresh and new. They sit quietly. Minds never stray. *Deutsche Sagen, Katz und Maus, Rotkäppchen,* and *Aschenputtel* read with passion ... inflection. They listen. They receive grounding ... direction.

Our children — I marvel at their intelligence and curiosity. They understand meaning and symbols in *Matushka's Galushkas* — children conquering soviet wrongs and evil mother punished. They listen intently to *River Bandit's Gold*. They ask about bounty, hard work, impossible dreams, realistic dreams, and hope.

While telling the tale of *The River Bandit*, Philomena, who is twelve, asked me about choices we make in life, about accepting responsibility for the consequences of our choices. She caught me unprepared. I stumbled through an answer. That night, I thought about my choices. I thought about responsibility.

I go to them because I need them.

America's Snare

Greta — small, helpless, mother-rabbit waits for someone to remove the bracelet that binds her. She waits for help. She wandered into a garden in a new world — a garden gushing with good things to eat — America's garden.

Father, Mother, and siblings stayed in old world. They stayed in the world they knew.

> She didn't want to go.
> She received a promise to bring her back.
> Promise made.
> She has a family in the new world.
> New family doesn't want to go back.
> Promise broken.
> Freedom — she had freedom.
> Freedom — she lost her freedom
> In America's snare.
> Wishing to be here,
> She is there.
> Friend in old world
> Wishing to be there —
> She is here.

Like Black Soot Thin

Like
Black soot thin
On clothes and skin,

Jealousy, anger, and hate,
Emotions not understood,
Blocking my vision
Like a hood.

Forgotten? Understood?

My image, my soul,
My life, my goal,
All of me,
They don't see.

Have the gods chosen my path?
Can I do more than pray?

My bad side
They don't see.
Change my attitude
For a better me.

Jealousy, anger, and hate,
Like black soot thin,
On my mind,
Clothes, and skin.

Intruders rejected.
Mind is free.
Forgotten and misunderstood —
I see.

Haircut By Half

November 1915

Dearest Emma, Anton, and Family,

Anna celebrated her twelfth birthday. She amazes and entertains us. She grew tall for her age and thin with her father's muscles. A mystery radiates from her that we can't explain. She splashes hope and inspiration on anyone near. A lovable, charming young girl that we call Anna Zee. She welcomes a fight and often her behavior becomes disobedi-ent, moody, reckless, and unpredictable. Sounds like Wolf, doesn't it? Anna Zee plays jokes on everyone, including her father and mother.

Anna Zee gives haircuts to the family. I don't remem-ber how this started, but she likes it. A few months ago, her father asked her to cut his hair. Wolf always reads the paper and pays no attention to the haircut. When Anna Zee finished, she quickly cleaned up and went for a walk. Your brother went about his chores. Nobody saw him until we sat down for supper. She cut the hair on one side of Wolf's head until almost bald. The other side she pretended to cut. We all enjoyed a good laugh, including Wolf. We call her, sometimes not so funny jokes — Anna-antics.

Strange to think a war could create something good. Apparently, the war created a worldwide shortage of wheat causing prices to rise. This year, we planted more acres in wheat than ever before. Wolf said Kansas produces more wheat than most countries. But even with this, I wish this war to end. Strange that our countries fight together — Russia, England, America. When the war ends, we may return home. I have not given up my dream, but Wolf remains a stubborn man.

Wishing to see you again,
Greta

Day Is Night

Our world bewilders, puzzles, and baffles us. Like the vampire bat, it hangs upside down.

In Solotoye, we hear of armies Russian, German, English, and American. We hear of armies Red and White. Who is wrong? Who is right? We don't know. Our men leave to fight. Most never return.

> Armies Red and White
> Wrong and Right
> Men leave to fight
> Day is night

Yesterday, the Tsar ruled Russia. Today, a traveler reported Bolsheviks killed Tsar Nicholas and his family. Nicholas, Alexandra, Olga, Tatiana, Maria, Anastasia, and Alexei are gone. WHY?

Blood drips from Russia's fangs.

NICHOLAS … ALEXANDRA … OLGA … TATIANA … MARIA … ANASTASIA … ALEXEI …

> Against a basement wall
> Young girl doesn't fall

Another for good measure
Search them for treasure

It drips.
Day is night.

Faces In A Window

Why did it happen? Why did I go there? Anton begged me to leave. Why did my mind slow everything, silence everything, except unintelligible barking of angry men — a muffled, garbled howling. I didn't hear the shots. I saw smoke from pistols — acrid trace.

Heinrich and Jacob in front of their house — parents, wives, and children inside. Men — everywhere shouting. I could see lips moving and gestures, but the words didn't come out. Bolshevik gangs demanding grain — all of it. Greta's brothers trying to keep a little — family to feed, seed. I stood on the ice cellar cover. I noticed the sun creeping over the roof of the stone house, two doves taking flight. I waited for the distinctive sound of their wings. Silence.

Guns appear. Pointed at chests. Dark clouds of smoke hang in the air. My friends slumped to the ground. No sound. Muted sound. Movement ceased. My eyes focused strangely, eerily, on stitching on Jacob's soiled pants — above the knee where Rosa mended a tear — Jacobs fist pounding dirt — then it stopped. I saw screaming faces in the window. I couldn't hear them. I did nothing. My mind failed me. I remember little more.

Faces in a window screaming
Dark smoke streaming
Mouths open wide
Sharp, white teeth cannot hide

Terrified eyes — I see only white
And doves frozen in flight

Anton picked me up and took me home.

Why couldn't I do something? I feel ashamed. I should have done ... something.

Visions haunt me now. Faces in that window return. I want to stop it, but don't know how. I don't recognize them. I pray the image to stop.

Prayers sent with no reply. I get no relief. Punishment it must be. Because I did nothing to stop them, you see.

... and took me home.

Home.

How can it ever be the same?

Brothers Heinrich And Jacob

March 1918

Greta,

Your parents asked that I write on their behalf. How do I begin? On Friday, 18 March, the Bolsheviks shot ... killed your brothers Heinrich and Jacob. I hesitate in providing more information, but you would certainly want to know why and how this happened. I grieve for you Greta and for your parents. They remain in shock. Their health slips away as sanity abandons our world.

As you know, the Bolsheviks demand that all grain from the country be sent to the cities where people starve. They shoot those who refuse. Heinrich and Jacob asked to keep enough for seed and to feed their families. They argued to protect their families. The angry men shot them. Your parents, your brothers' wives, and children watched in horror from the window. I'm sorry Greta.

This world continues to confuse us. In Solotoye, we thought the end of the war would bring sense and stability back into our lives. But Russia changes, a revolution the papers call it. Some thought the Bolsheviks would help farmers on the Volga. They steal. They murder. And now, armies within Russia fight each other. What happened to our world? My sincerest regrets and sympathy.

Emma

Helping Hands

I love his strong, capable, caring hands. A man's hands are sensual like his eyes or lips. Now that he ages, character replaces smooth boyish skin. I still feel warm inside when he holds my hand. He always helps the children and me. Helping hands find solutions to our problems. They push when needed, pull, lift, and caress. Hands on my waist as he stands behind me while I tend the stove — he doesn't know his hands there make problems melt like butter in the heavy black pan. Why don't I tell him?

They symbolize strength, experience, caring, and … well, many things I can't think of now.

Like me, he wears down. He mends his body to make it through another day — like we fix the old, failing, rusting plow.

What does he do for his mind?

Hands — cut and scarred in many places, rough, calloused, sweat mixed with dirt, yet soft like a whisper. They touch me without touching.

Beautiful, strong, caring hands — helping hands.

Pants . Shirts . Underwear

July 1923

Dear Zees, Greta, Bernard, Wolf, and Family,

The months vanish like leaves in fall — leaves that lose their beautiful colors, become brittle, and drop to the ground. Many years and leaves on the ground since I watched your wagons leave Solotoye. Sometimes, it feels as if you just left. Sometimes, it feels like forever. Sometimes, I don't want the feelings. It would be easier without, but then we forget. Don't we? I don't want to forget you. I prefer the pain.

I know you continue to write. I received your last letter long, long ago. Peter's two children, Birgeta and Rosa, died this year. How does a family deal with a child's death? How does our God, any god, let the children suffer? They get weak and die of many different illnesses. I'm sorry to burden you with our suffering.

Wolf and Greta, the money you sent has not reached the bank.

What the Russian government left undone with its idiotic plan of sending all grain to the cities — our weather completed. Our people die — mostly children and the old. We eat little, or ... nothing. Our clothes become rags. The angry famine continues into its third year. We barely manage to bury the dead. At times, the will and energy to do so abandons us. Guilt invades our minds as hunger ravages our bodies.

Amidst this horror — men, women, and children dying of hunger by the hundreds — lightning struck and killed a woman in Solotoye. At her burial, something strange happened. When Father mentioned that she died of a lightning strike, a man started laughing. Naturally, the few people there just watched — dazed at the sight and sound. The man fell to his knees, pounded the ground with his fists, and cried uncontrollably. He cursed God for letting this happen. Father didn't know what to do, so he simply closed his prayer book and walked away. Our world flaunts its insanity.

We try to take care of ourselves as we should. We try ... but we ... can't. The indignity of that becomes worse than the hunger, having no clothes, and no money to buy what we need. But even if we did have enough money, everything costs so much because of the war. One needs a pocketful of money to go to the market. I suppose we should not be concerned with that because the market has little to sell. The men and women strong enough to work the fields can do little with the remaining stock. The Bolsheviks took most of our stock. Many die from starvation. These poor animals become our food.

I don't know how much longer I will be able to write letters. We cannot afford paper, ink, and postage. Please continue writing even if your letters don't reach us. The soviet reads our mail. We must be careful. Maybe, I write *too much? But if they handle this job as well as their other tasks, why should we worry?*

This year the government opened a kitchen for children under fourteen years. They don't receive much. It's not the best food, but it's more than their parents can give them. The soviet tells us that anyone with family or friends in America should ask them for help. Zees and Greta, if you and my dearest brothers send money, send it to the German Market Bank in Katherinenstadt. If you send clothes or food, send it here. We mostly need pants, shirts, and underwear. Thank you.

About our trip to America, people from Solotoye continue trying to leave. Those that travel by train from Saratov get turned back before they reach Germany. We read in the paper about a priest that escaped to the south by sea. When we ask about our travel papers, the soviet tells us to check in a month or two. We must wait. We have no money for the papers. We have no food.

I remember, as small children, listening to a wonderful storyteller rambling about — a man in a red hat, a horse named Pull, a cat named Stay, and a wagon given the name Wagon. Boots got stuck in the mud, popped out, and ran to catch Wagon. I see holes in socks, toes wiggling and young girls giggling. Our children don't giggle anymore.

Wishing to see you again,
Emma and Anton

Like A Dark Painting

December 1923

To My Dearest Emma and Anton,

We grieve for the loss of your sweet grandchildren. The picture you paint of life in Solotoye reminds me of a somber oil landscape burdened with heavy strokes of gloomy greens, sunless blues, purples and blacks, so dense that when you study the painting looking for its message, its life, you can't see it — like the paintings in those old books with the weathered brown leather.

Many of our letters do not reach you in Solotoye, but we continue to write. Money was sent to the German Market Bank. We hope and pray that you receive the money and travel papers soon.

Organizations here and in Europe collect food and clothes for the poor people of our home country — Russia. We contribute much to these groups through our church in Ellis. I hope the food and clothing reach you quickly.

Emma, I hope the following helps lighten your soul.

One-half mile to the south of Stonewall, on the road to Ellis, the road runs into a big hill — not like the Volga Hills — smaller and without trees. The road turns to the left and then south again. We started calling this hill, Turn Hill, and now, all farmers around do the same. On the south side of Turn Hill, a little creek runs through a quiet, protected, beautiful meadow. When the creek runs high, the cows drink and cool themselves from summer's heat. We call this stream Cow Creek. The cows made a path around the hill. Sometimes, I lie in bed picturing our cows circling Turn Hill, never stopping, going around and around — silly behavior. So, we call this cow path ... well, we call it Cow Path, you know, like the wagon in Push's folktale.

Wishing to see you again,
Greta

The Outside Of Wrong

Soviet's Wrongs —

I bundle them like broken branches.

Tie them tight with rugged rope.

Cast them in the river.

Currents carry them away.

Watch. They disappear.

Wash my hands of it.

Smile. Celebrate.

I lie awake at night painting the image.

I must make it happen for our people.

I can't.

I sketch a child's drawing.

I know.

Soviet's Wrongs —

How do I measure the magnitude?

A thousand sins?

More than the drops of water in the oceans?

No.

There is WRONG.

What the soviet has done is OUTSIDE of wrong.

Soviet — Outside of Wrong.

Pure thoughts.

Tuesday Morning

Anton stole soviet ink and paper. He asked me to write about our starving children — to tell the world they die from hunger. One soiled piece of paper and little ink remain. I have little to say.

Tuesday morning, I dug for roots at the river. Weary eyes rested on a naked girl of seven or eight years lying upon the ground — her body so dirty the parched dusty soil welcomed her.

I went to her.

She held out a root. Her arm and hand, bone covered with skin, trembled.

Her protruding eyes asked me to take it. Too weak to eat, too frail to speak, her eyes held me.

I took it.

I covered her with my ragged shirt.

I lay beside her. I held her. I rocked her. My lips lingered on her brown cheek.

I felt her let go.

I carried her to the cemetery.

Tuesday morning.

Vanished

Like a bad magic trick, much of Solotoye has vanished. An unrecognizable Solotoye remains. Does anyone care? Would they know us? Do they understand our lives changed? Letters *from* family in America — we don't receive them anymore. Letters *to* our family in America — we can't afford ink, paper, and postage. The soviet burns letters — all of them. All of them?

Bernard, Zees, Wolf, Greta — do they think we disappeared? Do they think we died?

The Russian's want our land and our homes. They need our labor elsewhere. They tell us about work camps, but don't tell us where. They break up families. They let Anton stay because he makes furniture for them. He doesn't like it. He does it, so we stay together. If I blink, will we all be gone? If I turn my head, will they take another?

The soviet throws
A black cape over Solotoye.
We wait.
They jerk it away.
Like magic,
Gone.

Black Ink On Not-So-White Crumpled Paper

I pursue illusive *liquid grace* with black ink on not-so-white, crumpled paper. I didn't thank Anton for getting the soiled sheets. How do I capture and express my thoughts and emotions? I know one way — start writing. Search for the words I must write. Each blank page becomes an exploration. My goal — exercise imagination and reason. On these new paths, may I stumble upon discovery and wisdom.

Separation

As months turned into years, an unacknowledged acceptance of our reality settled over us like a heavy blanket on a cold winter's night, at times suffocating, yet, warm and comfortable. When rooster crowed, we pulled ourselves from under those heavy cloaks and made it through another day. Occasionally, a warm breeze visited our village carrying joy, hope, contentment, and pleasure. Yet, each day we returned to our beds and slipped under and behind our reality.

Twenty-seven years of separation from family and friends in America. What happened to those years? What happened during those years? How did we manage?

Hope fought many battles with despair and won most.

Contrasting emotions weaved themselves in and out of our lives during periods of —

Relative normalcy,
War,
Famine,
Deportation,
And we called it life.

Hope and despair,
Joy and sorrow,
Fear and contentment,
Pleasure and pain,
Affection and anger,
Surprise and disgust,

And we called it life.

Did I know at the train station in Warsaw that we would remain trapped in Russia? Is that why I stood over those tracks hypnotized by the cold, hard reality they represented? The most endearing trait a person can have is their ability to continue to fight — whatever the battle may be. That became my vow — take back my dignity, find and keep hope, continue the fight. Was I successful? I'm not the one to judge.

With each passing year, I wrote more poetry. I wrote fewer letters to America, aware of and puzzled by the fact, but did nothing to change it.

We received mostly good news from our family in

America, but two grave letters lamented the loss of Mother and Father. They died within a year of each other, Mother first, ten months after we returned from Warsaw. I think they knew.

We experienced joy and pain reading of the success of Stonewall Ranch. We wanted the best for them, but jealousy crawled in and warmed itself. Sometime during the war, I don't know why, I found a renewed interest in letters to family. I don't remember how long it lasted.

With each year, we shared more and more time with Greta's family. Strange circumstances separated Greta and me from our families. At some point, we both knew we would not see them, or each other, again. Maybe, that's when I renewed the letter writing. I don't remember.

What if this, what if that? Was there something more I could have done?

Inside A Sideways Second

I lie in warm protective bedding staring wildly into Solotoye's murky witching-hour, when a grammatical stranger
scratched on bedroom's frosted ebony-pane.

It slipped in.

I repeated the words haltingly. I tried to analyze the
uninvited phrase — time ... distorted time ... time is short
... trapped inside this abnormal temporal actuality ... life
twisted ... turned around ... sideways.

I tried thinking of other things ... affable, cheerful
things, but grave thoughts cloud my nights. Ideas, notions,
and images came and went in a hurried frantic storm. My
eyes focused on ... nothing. At times, they closed. Amid
shadowy frenzied thoughts, a mixture of new and old lines
invaded my consciousness. Reluctantly, I recognized them.
Mentally, I wrote verse.

Cold, dark night awake,
Beg the dawn to break.

Troubling thoughts get their way,
Welcome they overstay.
Come and go as they please,
Sanity they tease.

Beg the dawn to break.
More I cannot take.

Feel close walls.
They do not exist.
Strange words come,
I cannot resist.

Words repeated searching for sense —
Inside a sideways second ...
Foreign and no fence.

Mischievous mind sees no boundaries.
It takes its leave.
Reality flashes.
Fantasy and I grieve.

Wishing to see you again.
Writing poetry without pen.

Transparent reality,
Is what I see.

Like in spring's flood,
Words and lines rush by.
Eddies trap small, simple words.
Phrases pulled under and die.

Massive metal nails,
Young girls carry pails.

Seek the dawn.
I see no sign.
A sideways second —
A measure of time?

For a sideways second,
Reality flashes.
No rhyme, no reason,
It arrives — then dashes.

Faces in a window,
Images never stop.
Pants, shirts, underwear,
Needed just one crop.

Nicholas and family, shot.
Bolsheviks, a scourge, blot.

My Christmas gift,
Ten hands up,
Hold the thoughts.
Shatter like a cup.

Like debris in spring's flood,
Caught in a vortex, or rushing by.
Beg the dawn to break. I cry.

I plead ... for sanity's sake.
Light, only a hint,
Welcomed purple tint.

I rise. I go to the glass —
A visual echo.
I daub icy tears.
They remain.

Hands on sill, head on glass, I
Lean.
Inside a sideways second ...
What does it
Mean?

Trucks At Night

January 1930
Greta Zees and w

sorry. writing is bad   hands shake.

I hope you can read   you get this

A terrible thing
took Anton. Treat us like animals men came

trucks at night   guns

don't know where he is
his eyes   hands held onto

screamed and cursed

He's gone
find him   get stronger.
see his eyes in dreams   will leave   find him tomorrow.
Trucks ... at night

Emma

Scattered Papers

Slowly, I gather sundry empty ink bottles and broken pens. I peer into the laden wicker basket wondering why I kept them. Cleared family table — my worktable. Pens placed in bottles and set on cold, smooth, wooden planks. Some bottles remain empty. Spent writing tools moved deliberately around stained boards — moved until the image pleases my eye. I touch bottles and table's familiar blemishes of ink, spilled food, and drink — a silent painful parting. I placed Anton's tools on his workbench. Saws, hammers, and drills — ink bottles, paper, and featherless quills — all will stay. Tools tell our story.

Lungs plead as I scatter papers throughout our home — on dusty forlorn furniture, on neglected floors. I open all windows and doors. I summon air currents to ferry yellowed wrinkled papyrus.

Imitation rains will dampen thin paper leafs as they lie upon receptive soil. Writer's paint will blur. It will run. Words will be washed. I wish I could have done better — done more. Imitation rains — please soak the earth with my words. I want to leave a mark on this land — this place.

I tried to write words that work hard like the people of Solotoye, that sing and dance, leap and fall, maybe crawl, or stand still like quiet trees, tall — words that elicit wonder, surprise, question, and provoke. I wanted to use these expressions to turn wrinkled and ironed thoughts into images, sounds, and rhythm.

I fell in love with language. I explored its depths and studied its complexities. I wanted to solve its mysteries. Alas, like a cat, I scratched in tall grass searching for an elusive grasshopper. Language engaged and entertained me. But I walk away hungry.

Letters to family and friends in America — my petition, please, read them to the children. Help them to remember, to discover *family* that lived in a far away place in Russia — a place of meadowlark songs — a place of forgotten wrongs. It's my request — a wish for my papers in America.

I pause at the gate. My mind paints a final, arresting image — background of house and farmyard dressed in blacks, grays, and brown. Papers scattered — covering the ground. A solitary, white, wind-blown furled-sheet is right-of-center, so conspicuous, so extended, it almost falls off the imaginary canvas. Black, protruding words form lines that run laterally to the end of that bright-white paper, some turn unexpectedly, but not aimlessly.

Blanched, populated page
Suspended for all to see.
Resident letters, like a, b, m and e,
Suspended for all to see.

Working words, lines, images,
For all to see.

I turn. I will myself to take short, painful steps. Little strength. I hear papers rustling. A faint smile momentarily transforms my troubled countenance.

I don't look back.

Smiling, I imagine papers taking flight. Inside, something familiar stirs. Thoughts soar ... they glide ... answers alight.

I know why ...

Why the papers must be carried by the winds. Why Solotoye's soil must be marked.

I know.

I don't look back.

218

Shadows

I don't know where they took him. I will ask everyone on River Road if they saw Anton. Did you see a handsome man with a graying black mustache? His name is Anton ... Anton Wasen. I will tell them I am Emma, his wife. He has a mustache and hands that ... He knelt awkwardly, painfully in the back of an open truck. Hands ... grasped the metal end-gate as if trying to hold onto his world, as if praying, wanting to help, but unable. Sorrowful, speaking eyes cried their ... Good Bye. They held me until ...

Did you see him? Please, did you see him?

I begin. One painful step — then two. A cumbersome coat, porous boots, and ragged hat accompany me. Keep gloved hands in coat pockets, I tell myself. Look, holes. Stop and rest.

Wiggens' Place ...

Tavern's gate ...

Something, something,

And be late.

I will sit in the tavern. Tables and benches — who took them? Why haven't they repaired the roof? I sit on cold creaking steps. Greta and I sat over there. We were young. When did I get this hole in my glove? A whimsical walkway — he built it this way on purpose. Push Wiggens. Where are you Push Wiggens? Stay died ... many years ago. Didn't you know?

I have to go on. Close the gate. It doesn't latch. They took him this way — north towards ... beyond ...

... Solotoye's sepulcher that shelters dormant, graying steppe-grass. The baneful plant shrouds scattered wooden crosses and markers that ... lean, are broken, or sleep on earth's frosted mantle. I must say goodbye to my children. They rest here ... somewhere ... what shall I say?

I'm leaving Solotoye.

Anton, I'm tired. I love you. I'm sorry Anton ... for not being stronger ... for not stopping them. I did nothing Anton. Once again, I did nothing.

I hold your hands. Eyes close ... to remember. You give me freedom, strength, and love. You understand me ... you are gone.

I don't look back because all are gone.

Corporeal shadows,
Sketched in charcoal gray
By morning's weak winter-sun,
Stretched on snow-covered way.

Shallow, brittle, fleeting imprints
Of craven pillagers guide us.
I stand delicate like carriage marks.

Naked, raven-hued, silent trees,
Forsaken, exhausted, silent fields
Stand delicate like carriage marks.

I shiver sensing Matushka's icy tongue
Crying, calling my name.
Steppe's frigid, fatal wind bites
Exposed, venerable sheath.

Faint, cloudy presence ...

Faint, cloudy presence,
Sketched in charcoal gray
By morning's weak winter-sun,
Stretched on snow-covered way.

Carriage marks
In shadows' sight.
A simple quest,
Destination ... Right.

In shadows' sight,
Dignity, hope ...
Right.

SOLOTOYE

APPENDIX

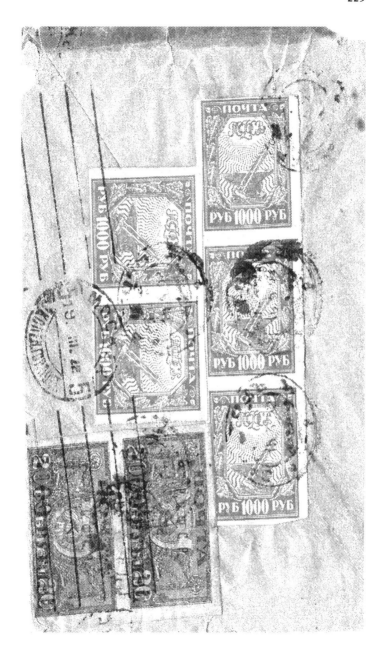

Envelope sent by Helena Haas Miller

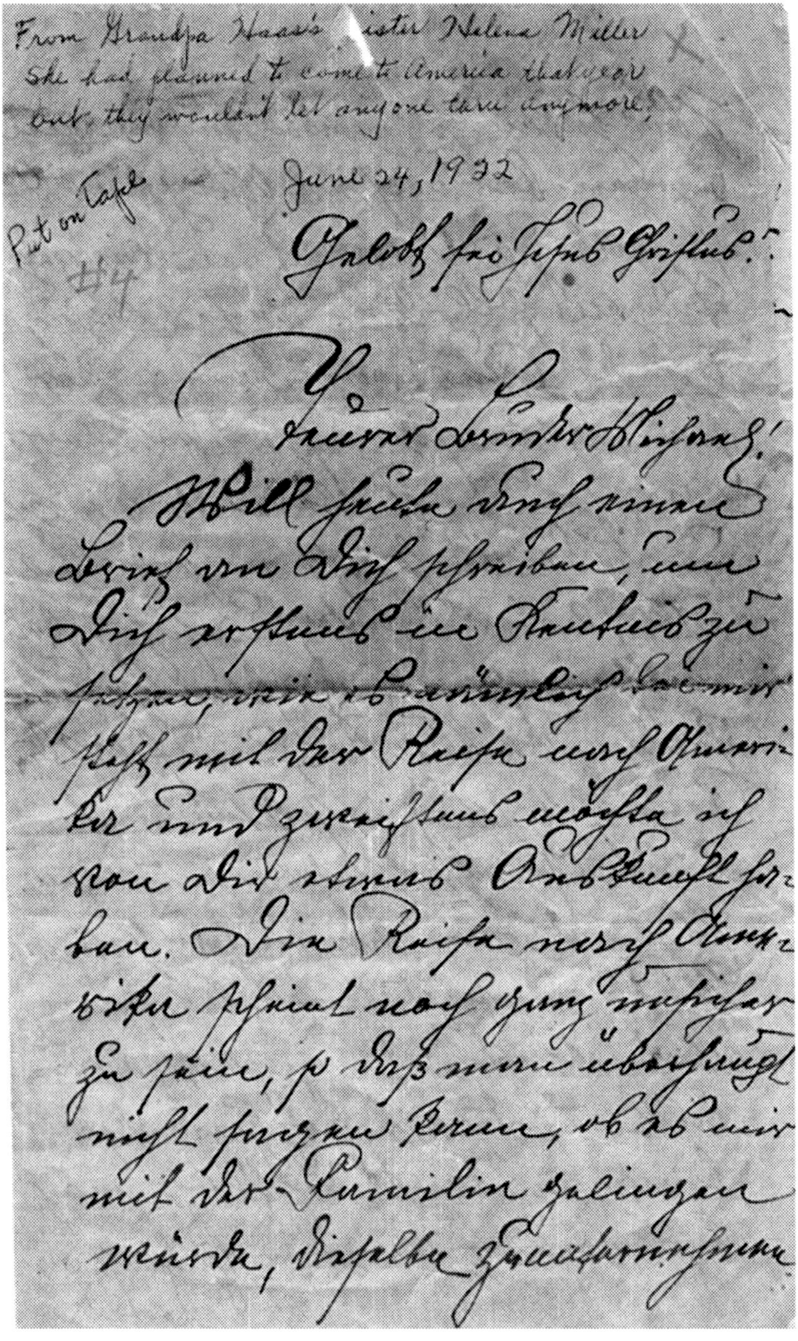
From Grandpa Haas's sister Helena Miller
She had planned to come to America that year
but they wouldn't let anyone leave anymore.

Put on Tape
#4

June 24, 1932

Gelobt sei Jesus Christus!

Teurer Bruder Michael!
Will heute doch einmal
Brief an Dich schreiben, um
Dich erstens einmal zu
fragen, wie es nämlich bei mir
steht mit der Reise nach Ameri-
ka und zweitens möchte ich
von Dir etwas Auskunft haben. Die Reise nach Ame-
rika scheint noch ganz unsicher
zu sein, so daß man überhaupt
nicht sagen kann, ob es mir
mit der Familie gelingen
würde, dieselbe Zusammenkunft

Letter from Helena Haas Miller

erhalten haben ich noch nichts, kein
Geld und auch keinen Angerechten
Schreiben aber schon viele Danke
Sagen bekommen, auch die Quittung
habe noch nichts erhalten. —
Gesund bin ich mit meiner ganzen
Familie, alle sind für jetzt noch
munter und wohlauf. Nun grüße
wir dich mit der schwachen Aus-
sicht Euere jungen Kinder
grüßen euch von uns meine
beiden Anton und Jakobele
mit ihrer Familie, auch die
Marthe und schwager Georg
mit ihren Kindern. Nun
will ich schließen, sind alle
dem göttlichen Schutz mach-
end verbleibe ich Euer
treuer Jakob mit Kinder

24. Juni 1922.

The Crusaders for Law and Order
Courtesy of The Ellis Review, Ellis KS

Michael Haas Jr. Family circa 1914

**Katherina and Michael Haas Jr.
with daughter Katherina**

In memory of:

Helena and Ferdinand
Katherina and Michael, Jr.
Rosa and Anton
Anna and Jacob
Katherina and Michael, Sr.
Joseph and Jacob
and
to all Volga Germans that died in Russia

"This Parting Was Well Made."

Out of my sight! Thou dost infect mine eyes.

Would that my tongue were in the thunder's mouth!
Then with a passion would I shake the world.

My tongue will tell the anger of my heart,
Or else my heart, concealing it, will break,
And rather than it shall, I will be free
Even to the uttermost, as I please, in words.

And whether we shall meet again I know not.
Therefore our everlasting farewell take:
For ever, and for ever, farewell, Cassius!
If we do meet again, we shall smile;
If not, why then, this parting was well made.

(from King Richard III, King John, Taming of the Shrew,
and Julius Caesar – as compiled in Robin P. Williams'
book, *Sweet Swan of Avon: Did a Woman Write Shakespeare?*)

Thank you Robin
Thank you Mary Sidney